MW00884477

PRAISE FOR THE BESTSELLING NOVELS OF KAREN FENECH

NOVELS BY KAREN FENECH

Betrayal

Gone

Unholy Angels

Imposter: The Protectors Series — Book One

Snowbound: The Protectors Series — Book Two

Pursued: The Protectors Series — Book Three

Hide: The Protectors Series — Book Four

Three Short Stories Of Suspense: Deadly
Thoughts, Secrets & The Plan

HIDE

The Protectors Series — Book Four

KAREN FENECH

For Andrew

CHAPTER ONE

It was now or never. Allison Sandoval took one last glance over her shoulder. The ballroom was crowded on this Saturday evening, filled with the dignitaries and diplomats who'd gathered to honor her husband, Rafael, on his last night on U.S. soil. In the morning, he'd be flying back to his native South America. But he'd be leaving without her.

Rafael was tall and the height advantage gave him a wide view of the room, but the crowd around him was thick. Allison had been slowly working her way from his side. At any other time, it would be impossible for her to take more than a step away. He, or one of the men Rafael publicly called her bodyguards but who were in reality her jailers, always pulled her back. But the men around Rafael tonight were as tall as he was and Allison took the opportunity to blend in with those milling around him.

Her grip on the champagne flute stretched the

skin tight across her hands as she forced herself to move slowly, not to make a mad dash for the exit. She was sweating. Could feel perspiration trickling down her neck, left bare with her hair swept up into an intricate style, and continuing down her spine beneath the flowing silver gown.

At the door, an elderly man was making his way into the room. He held the door open and Allison walked by him into the hall. With regret, she bypassed the coat check. Her dress had sleeves that covered her arms, but the late October air was cold. She'd been out of the States for six months and in the South American heat. She'd forgotten how cool the nights could get in New York at this time of year and this year, this part of the state was experiencing unusually frigid weather. Didn't matter. She would not retrieve her coat. The place was crawling with security people who missed nothing. She could not risk anyone suspecting she was about to leave the building.

She'd almost reached one of the Ladies' rooms on this level of the luxury hotel. Earlier, when she'd accompanied Rafael on a tour of the building, she'd taken note of where the washrooms were located, seeking one that wasn't at the end of a corridor. What she'd found wasn't ideal, but she'd make do. She chose the restroom that provided the best access.

She turned down that corridor and kept walking. A door at the end of the hall led to a staircase. She made her way down the six flights. Her heels clicked against the steps, echoing in the stairwell, and she glanced back over her shoulder, fearing she would give herself away. But no one came charging through the door after her.

Rather than take the exit that opened to the lobby, she continued down to the underground garage. There would be a way to the street from there and freedom.

She dropped the glass of champagne she was still holding in a garbage can and left the hotel. The cold air hit her and while it stole her breath, it was also bracing. She was a long way from being free yet, but it was the closest she'd come since marrying Rafael. The last months had been horrific. Tears sprang to her eyes. She blinked them back but some still fell. She swiped them away, angry with herself for going back there. For allowing Rafael to torture her even though she wasn't with him. She had been strong before. She would be again. She would not let that pain and fear defeat her. As hard as he'd tried, Rafael hadn't broken her. Her eyes stung with tears again and again she forced them back. Her life was not the only one that depended on her getting away from Rafael.

A woman turned to look at her. Allison couldn't afford to be noticed, to have anyone recall she'd passed this way. She stepped out from beneath the street lights, went into the shadows cast by the tall buildings and increased her step as much as she was able.

What she really needed to do was to stop and lean against one of the buildings. She was so tired. It was a struggle to remain on her feet. The small burst of strength she'd mustered to make her escape had waned. She was breathing hard, a combination of her body's weakness and terror. It was the terror that kept her moving. She couldn't be caught. If Rafael found her ... For an instant, fear cut off her breath. No, she would not be caught and taken back to Rafael. She had to finish this with him. *She could not fail.*

She didn't know how long she'd walked, dragging her feet, when the tall buildings gave way to smaller structures spaced wider apart. Traffic, both pedestrian and vehicular, was thin here. One of the small buildings looked to be a factory of some kind. Whatever it was, the place looked deserted for the weekend. Could she spend the night there? Did she dare stop moving?

The place would be locked but it was possible she could find something in the alley beside the building to break a window. She winced at doing that but as she shivered in the bitter cold, she tamped down on her conscience.

Moonlight lit her way into the alley. She bent and got down on the ground. She spotted a wine bottle, minus the cap. Would the bottle be enough to break the window? She wasn't sure, but she had to try.

She was about to reach for it, then curled her fingers into her palms. When she reached out would she find she was mistaken and the bottle wasn't there, that there wasn't any bottle at all? She couldn't always trust what her own eyes told her. She closed them briefly, afraid this would be one of those times. But, no. When she forced herself to reach out, her fingers closed around the neck of the bottle. Her pulse sped up.

Allison left the alley. It was a weekend. No one

should be back to work in that building before Monday. Still, she hesitated. She couldn't afford to make a wrong move. If she came upon someone police would be called. Then Rafael. Fear had the back of her neck prickling.

No lights were on inside the building. The building did look closed up tight. She could barely keep herself upright now in her exhaustion. Her body swayed toward it but she didn't take a step. She remained where she was. She faced her reality. As much as she needed somewhere to sleep and to hide for the night, even if the door was wide open, she couldn't go into that dark place.

She closed her eyes at her weakness, fighting back tears. She was now shaking and huddling into herself in a futile attempt to get warm. She went back into the alley, to the small alcove dug into the side of the building, and went as deep inside it as she could.

* * *

Zach Corrigan was sleeping when the monitor beeped, signaling the secure perimeter around his place had been breached. He was instantly awake and on full alert. He rolled onto his side and punched buttons on the small panel in the wall, bringing up a view of the outside. He owned a large stretch of isolated land in Blake County, New York. A long, unnamed dirt road, bordered by trees, led only to Zach's place. Anyone on this road would be coming to see him. Moonlight provided excellent light tonight, making the lights around the place unnecessary. Zach's house came into view, a big ranch-style, as did the extension off the main house that served as the base of operations for his organization. Behind was a huge pond, currently frozen over. The cameras he had set up at strategic points on the grounds showed several views of the place. Zach would see his visitors long before they reached his front door.

The vehicle making its way to him was a limousine and though the occupant likely had no idea he or she was being monitored, there was no attempt to conceal the approach. An assassin wouldn't announce his arrival.

It was just shy of two in the morning on a Sunday. Zach's business didn't run nine to five and late callers weren't unusual. But if this were one of Zach's government contacts coming to his door about a mission, they would have called first. Zach's line of work made it essential that he be cautious. He made no apology for it.

He tracked the progress of the limousine. Decided to let it proceed. If he'd misjudged his visitor, he'd soon rectify that.

He slept naked and now put on jeans and a T-shirt. His gun was on his nightstand, always ready. He secured it at his back, under the shirt, then left the bedroom.

A coffee maker was on a timer set to start at seven a.m. He got the machine going. As the rich aroma of the strong dark brew filled the air, the monitor beeped again, this time to indicate a presence on his driveway.

Zach called up the images on the kitchen

monitor. Two men emerged from the limousine. One was built like a brick, clearly muscle for someone, but he stood against the hood of the black car, making no attempt to follow or shield the other man who moved briskly to Zach's front door and rang the bell.

Zach filled a mug of coffee for himself and drank a bit before going to the door to meet his visitor. He opened the door and checked out the muscle. The guy hadn't moved from the limo. He stood with his arms folded at his chest, his hands tucked under his arms to ward off the cold.

Zach focused on the man in front of him. His cashmere coat flapped in the breeze. The wind put color in his cheeks that were sallow and drawn. His eyes looked heavy from lack of sleep. "Help you?"

"Are you Zachary Corrigan?"

Zach clocked the man at around his own age—early thirties. The guy had an accent. South American. Zach had spent enough time in that region to be able to pinpoint exactly where on the continent his visitor was from. This man was from a remote area. Zach had learned of a diplomatic visit to the U.S. from the country's leader in a bid to secure financial aid. That leader was Rafael Sandoval, the man now standing here with Zach.

"I'm Corrigan," Zach said.

The man extended a gloved hand. The leather was of the finest, soft as melted butter.

"I am Rafael Sandoval," he said. "Mr. Corrigan. I need your help."

Sandoval's expression was earnest and

desperate. Zach stepped back from the door and led the other man to the kitchen.

Zach topped up his mug. "Coffee?"

"No, thank you."

The man didn't look like he needed the caffeine. He looked about to jump out of his skin. Zach leaned back against the dark counter. In addition to jobs for Uncle Sam, Zach's organization also took on work from other countries and from private clients. "Who sent you to me?"

"Roger Morse told me about you," Sandoval said.

Sandoval named one of Zach's government contacts. "What do you need my help with?"

"Mr. Morse does not know the reason I have come to you," Sandoval added.

Zach narrowed his eyes. "Which is?"

"Before I begin, I must confirm that you are a military man."

Zach kept his gaze on Sandoval, wondering where this was going. "I'm sure you already got from Morse that I was a SEAL."

Sandoval let out a long breath. "I am also a military man. There is a code of honor among us. I need to ask for your utmost discretion."

"Why don't you tell me what this is about?"

Sandoval's shoulders slumped then he straightened his posture. "I need you to find my wife."

"I'm not a PI." Zach wasn't going to elaborate on what his organization did. His contracts for the government were classified, sending him and his people into places in all parts of the world where others couldn't or wouldn't go. He maintained the same level of confidentiality for the jobs he took from private clients.

"I do not need an investigator," Sandoval said. "I need someone with your skills and your discretion. I am here in your country in an attempt to secure aid for mine. I cannot let word about my wife's disappearance become front page news. I cannot allow the focus to shift away from my country's very real need. This is a personal matter. My wife, Allison, and I were attending a gathering in my honor yesterday evening. It was to be our last night in your country. We were to fly home this morning. One moment Allison was standing at my side and the next she was gone. I confess I was distracted. An agreement with your country would mean so much to mine." Sandoval rubbed his gloved hand back and forth across his brow with what appeared to be enough force to shred skin. "I was not paying enough attention to Allison."

Zach leaned forward. "If your wife was abducted—"

"No. She was not abducted." Sandoval squeezed his eyes shut so tightly the skin at the corners puckered. "She walked away."

Zach pushed off the counter. "Unless your wife is a minor, she's perfectly free to come and go as she pleases. There's nothing I can do for you."

Sandoval rubbed his brow hard again. "Obviously, she is of legal age. You do not understand. She must be found."

Zach repeated his earlier statement. "I'm not a

PI. I can recommend a good investigator though I'm not sure you need one. You have your own people to look for her, my government and law enforcement would also look for her. You don't need me."

"My wife is delicate. Fragile. Law enforcement and government agencies would overwhelm her when they find her. She must be handled gently." Sandoval withdrew his wallet and from it a photograph he held out to Zach. "This is Allison."

Zach glanced at the picture without taking it. The woman was a stunner. Waves of blond hair fell to her shoulders. Big eyes in a deep green rather than the blue he expected to go along with all that fair hair. She was dolled up and dressed to the nines in what looked like a pose for a State photo—wife of the country's new president. Zach raised his gaze from the picture and back to Sandoval. "This isn't the type of work my organization handles."

Sandoval ran a shaking hand back through his hair. "My wife is not a well woman."

The idea of an ill woman out on the streets without help didn't sit well with Zach, but if she were sick, why would she leave? There had to be a reason Allison Sandoval had left her husband. Zach eyed Sandoval and asked him straight out. "Why'd she leave you?"

"It was not deliberate. Allison wandered away from the ballroom last night. She does that if I do not keep a close watch on her."

Zach crossed his arms. "What aren't you telling me?"

Sandoval's face drew tight in an expression of pain. "My wife suffers from delusions, hallucinations and paranoia. She cannot determine what is real from what is imagined. She is on medication but she has been gone since last night and has been without it. And it is so cold to be outside. She must be found now. She will not survive long on her own."

Zach frowned. Clearly, the woman needed to be found quickly. He had no doubt he could do that and a lot faster than if he sent Sandoval on his way to find someone else to do the job. It wasn't his usual recovery mission but Allison Sandoval needed to be recovered. Zach addressed Sandoval. "I'll find her."

CHAPTER TWO

After Sandoval left, Zach took out his cell phone and called his second-in-command. Despite the time, Gavin Chase answered at once with a cheery, "What's up, boss?"

"Got a job," Zach said.

"Who do you want for it? I'll round them up."

"It's not something that requires the team. I have this one, but I need you to run a check on the guy who hired us. South American named Rafael Sandoval. His country's been in and out of the news in the last year. Sandoval's father, the president and dictator, died about a year back and Sandoval has taken up the reins."

"Yeah, I read about this guy. He says with his father's death he wants to put an end to the old ways. Wants to democratize the country. He's been in talks here about doing that. What does he need us for?"

"It's a personal matter. His wife left him. She wandered off. She's not well and needs to be found now. I told him I'd find her. Get on this right away, Chase."

"You got it."

Zach showered and dressed and by the time he left his bedroom, Chase was back on the phone.

"I found a newspaper photo of him and a hot blonde," Chase said. "The photo accompanied an engagement announcement. Wife, Allison, maiden name, Kent, is from D.C. She was a school teacher. Both parents still living. One sibling, a sister. Allison met Sandoval a year ago while she was taking her fifth graders on a tour of the White House and he was on his first diplomatic visit."

Chase added background and current information on Sandoval, including the hotel where Sandoval was staying, though Zach knew for security reasons Sandoval's location would be kept confidential and not be disclosed to the media or the public. That hadn't stopped Chase from finding out.

Chase provided details of Sandoval's accommodation and who, among his personal staff and bodyguards, were traveling with him.

"No red flags, Zach," Chase concluded. "Nothing on him."

It was a routine check Zach never overlooked with a new client. He didn't like surprises. "I'll be in touch."

Zach ended the call. Allison Sandoval had been missing for some time. He needed to find her.

* * *

Allison had remained huddled into herself throughout the night. Her muscles had stiffened from bunching them as tightly as she could in an attempt to combat the cold and from the cold itself. The alcove had cut some of the wind but could do nothing to dispel the bitter chill of the air.

It was now dawn. Rafael was supposed to fly home this morning. She had no illusions her escape would be that easy. That he'd just leave and she was free. She couldn't afford to stay put any longer. She had to get moving. She had a destination in mind. Once she reached it, she'd truly be free.

Her stomach growled. She didn't know when she'd last eaten. Her throat was parched. These discomforts were bearable. She'd endured so much worse. Once she got to where she was going, there'd be food there. She'd eat then. She could wait until then.

She put her hand out, pushed off the brick and exited the alcove. A gust of wind blew into the alley. She shivered and hunched her shoulders. She moved as quickly as she was able, driven by the cold and by her desperate need to get where she was going. By the time she reached the end of the alley, she was almost running. She turned onto the sidewalk and collided with a man on his way into the alley.

"Mrs. Sandoval!"

She hit the man squarely in the chest that was rock-hard and took her breath with the force of the impact. She would have landed on the ground but his hands came up to steady her. Big hands like the rest of him. His body was all muscle, solid. In another lifetime she would have appreciated how good the man looked but right now her stomach clenched at hearing her name on his lips and all she could think was that he was formidable. She looked up at him. He had piercing eyes in his handsome face and those eyes looked as hard as the rest of him.

"Mrs. Sandoval," he repeated.

She had to get away. She brought her knee up. The man dodged the blow easily. His grip on her tightened, not enough to hurt but enough to remove any notion that she could get away from him.

"I'm not going to hurt you. My name is Zach Corrigan. I'm here to help you. Your husband sent me to find you and take you back to him."

The man—Zach—took one hand from her, unclipped his cell phone from his belt and held it out to her.

"Call your husband to verify he sent me," Zach said. "I won't hurt you. All I want is for you to be back with him safe again."

Allison's throat closed. Her chest tightened and she couldn't breathe. She wouldn't go back to Rafael. She began to fight this man with everything she had in her.

Zach tightened his hold, pinning her arms. "You don't know me and you have every reason to be cautious, but the truth here is I outweigh you by about seventy pounds and top you by a foot. If I wanted to force you to accompany me, you'd already be in my vehicle. Please. Call your husband."

Allison shook her head. "You can't take me back to Rafael. I can't go back to him."

"Your husband is worried about you. I'm here to help you."

"Please. *Please*. If you really want to help me, then let me go."

* * *

Allison Sandoval looked very different from the photo Zach had seen—a shell of the woman in the picture. Traces of her beauty were there, but despite the liberal application of cosmetics, her skin was pale, her eyes too huge in her face that was now far too thin. Her hair was done up, showing the delicate bones in her cheeks and jaw, and long glittering fake earrings that matched the rest of the fake jewelry she was decked out in. Jewelry that looked too heavy for her. Her fine gown hung on her skinny body. The woman looked ravaged by her illness. No wonder Sandoval was so desperate to find her.

Despite the change in her appearance, Zach found he was unable to look away from her. She looked terrified but there was more than fear. Her mouth was pressed tightly in anger and defiance. The woman had fight in her. She was not the meek woman he'd expected. It made him wonder what Allison Sandoval had been like before she became ill. Zach would bet she'd been a lot more than just a pretty face.

Allison strained against his hold. Despite the fact that she was doing her best to break away from him, he lightened his grip. The woman felt like she'd break under his hands.

She glanced at his phone—at him—as if he were a snake. How to reassure her? "I'll help you," he said softly. He held her gaze and nodded once slowly.

"By taking me back to Rafael?" Her eyes flashed in anger. "That isn't helping me. Rafael will kill me."

Her words shook Zach. He reminded himself what Sandoval had said about her mental condition. That she suffered from paranoia. "No one is going to kill you. Your husband wants you safe."

He was still offering his phone. She still made no move to take it and he returned it to his belt. The woman was trembling and not just from fear but from the cold. Her dress was long and had sleeves but the material gave no insulation from the biting wind.

"You're freezing," he said gently. Keeping one hand on her, he removed his jacket. With his free hand, he draped it around her. It fit him to the waist but fell below her knees. He didn't know if she was even aware he'd placed it on her. She continued to watch him as if she thought he might pounce on her. He knew how to incite fear but he didn't want that now. He didn't want Allison to be afraid of him. It was time they got moving. "My vehicle isn't far. Let's get you out of the cold."

She made a sound of distress. "I won't be going with you." Her words came fast. Her voice was harsh with terror. "I'll continue on my own."

He couldn't let her do that. "No reason to. Let

me help you." He wasn't sure if he'd be able to get through to her, given what Sandoval had told him about her mental state. "This way to my vehicle."

"Just turn your back and let me walk away. I know Rafael must be paying you a lot of money to take me back but I'll find a way to repay you. Just, please, let me go."

The woman was begging him and her pleading got to him but he couldn't let himself act on it. She wasn't in a position to determine what was best for herself. He had to harden himself against her pleas. She wasn't well. "I can't do that and it isn't because of the money. I can't in good conscience let you go off on your own."

She laughed then, a harsh bitter sound. "Conscience? You work for Rafael, you have no conscience."

Zach didn't respond. He took a step but she dug in her heels. He could force her to move of course, or scoop her into his arms and move her himself. No, he'd just let her be. He unclipped his phone once again and made the call to Sandoval.

Sandoval arrived quickly. The limousine pulled up to the curb. Sandoval waited for the driver to round the car and open the door for him, then slowly stepped out.

Allison looked at Sandoval and shuddered. Zach still had one hand on her and felt it. Her eyes became opaque with terror and then a look of resignation and hopelessness filled them that kicked Zach in the gut.

Sandoval nodded to the muscle who served as his driver and the man took Allison by the elbow.

Zach realized he was still holding her and released her. The driver led her to the car where she disappeared behind the tinted glass.

"Mr. Corrigan," Sandoval said.

Zach forced himself to look away from the limo and to the man.

"I will be taking my wife home tonight," Sandoval said. "Goodbye."

Sandoval withdrew an envelope bulging with cash from inside his coat and held it out to Zach. When Zach didn't reach for it, Sandoval tossed the envelope at Zach's feet. That done, he returned to the limousine and the vehicle drove away.

CHAPTER THREE

Zach watched Sandoval's limousine become a speck in the distance and then disappear. He continued to stare at where the limo had been for some time. Finally, he shook his head and rubbed the back of his neck. There was no more reason for him to be here.

A garbage truck pulled up to a Dumpster in the alley that had temporarily housed Allison Sandoval. Zach left Sandoval's envelope on the ground and made his way to his SUV.

Zach floored the gas pedal, anxious to be gone from this place. He put miles between himself and that alley, but he couldn't get Allison Sandoval and the haunted look in her eyes out of his mind. He needed something else to think about. He had work to do back at his place. The next mission to plan. But his mind wasn't on business. His lips twisted sourly. Right now, the last thing he wanted to think about was what he did for a living. When he found himself on the road to Mitch's place, he went with it.

It wasn't until Mitch came to the door in jeans with the top snap open and no shirt, his hair mussed and his eyes heavy with sleep that Zach realized just how early it was on a Sunday morning.

"Zach?" Mitch's gaze cleared. That fast the sleepy look was gone. "Everything okay?"

Mitch Turner was Blake County's chief of police and the closest thing to a brother Zach had. Mitch, his brother Ben, Gage Broderick, Ryan Crosby and John Burke were family to Zach who'd never had any before these men. Zach rubbed a hand back through his hair. "Sorry, man. I didn't think how early it was. I'll let you get back to sleep."

Mitch stepped back from the door. "I'm good. Come in. I'll get breakfast going."

Zach followed Mitch down the hall to the kitchen. The house was quiet but for the hum of the central heating. Zach glanced at the stairs as he passed them.

"Shelby and Sara must still be upstairs," Zach said, lowering his voice.

Shelby was Mitch's bride of seven weeks and Sara was Shelby's three-year-old from a previous relationship.

"Yeah. Sara climbed into our bed and she and her mom are fast asleep." Mitch smiled. "I'm talking to a lawyer tomorrow morning. I'm starting adoption proceedings."

Zach knew Mitch was crazy about the little girl. "That's great."

Mitch went to the fridge and took out eggs,

bacon, hash brown potatoes, and bread. "Shelby was up late making party plans for when the adoption is final. She showed me a bunch of pictures for flowers and asked me which ones I liked. They're flowers." Mitch's eyes widened and his mouth gaped in a look of utter helplessness. "They all look the same to me."

Zach grinned as he leaned back against one wall. "I hear women are big on that kind of thing."

Mitch reached into the drawer under the stove and pulled out a couple of frying pans. "Yeah. She hasn't ever been able to kick back and be happy with Sara. Be happy at all." He shook his head. "I'll wear the damn flowers myself if it will help make this perfect for her."

Mitch became pensive. Zach believed Mitch had gone back to the day, two months earlier, when he'd nearly lost Shelby to her own brother's bullet. If Shelby had died, a part of Mitch would have surely died, too. Zach had no experience with love like that. Love like Sandoval had for Allison?

Zach didn't want to think of Allison Sandoval and the way she'd looked when he'd left her but his stomach tightened. Feeling edgy, he pushed off the wall, got the coffee maker going, then took two mugs from a cupboard and filled them. He placed one on the counter beside Mitch and took his own to the breakfast bar.

Mitch picked up his mug and took a swallow. "When are you shipping out?"

"I haven't mapped out our next assignment." Zach hesitated, then got angry with himself for doing that. He had nothing to be hesitant about. "I did a quick job this morning."

"Oh?"

Zach swirled the coffee in his mug. "A guy looking for his missing wife."

Mitch set strips of bacon into one pan, potatoes in another. "Not your usual thing."

"We recover people. This situation wasn't that different."

"I hear a 'but' coming."

Zach and Mitch went back to boyhood. If anyone could read Zach, Mitch could. "Something about this whole set up isn't adding up for me. Fuck, Mitch, I'm questioning if I read this wrong."

Mitch turned away from the stove to Zach, giving him his full attention. "How so?"

The bacon and potatoes hissed and popped in the pans and only that sound could be heard for a moment. It wasn't like Zach to second-guess himself but then he'd never doubted himself when it came to a job.

He ended the silence and met Mitch's gaze. "I met with the guy about the recovery, and he said his wife wasn't well. That she suffered from mental illness. When I found the woman, she begged me not to return her to her husband. I went with what the husband told me about her, but this whole thing doesn't feel right in my gut. Their reunion was off."

Mitch frowned. "Tell me about it."

Zach released an impatient breath then began to pace the room. The coffee in the mug he still held sloshed to the rim. "The guy—the husband—was a basket case when he came to me about his wife's disappearance but when he got her back?" Zach shook his head. "Nothing. He didn't so much as look at her before he turned her over to his driver. Doesn't mesh with the guy I met at my place."

Mitch regarded Zach as he moved around the room. "If he was torn up when you saw him, then it doesn't sound like he's the kind not to show his emotions."

"No, it doesn't. And the look in his wife's eyes when I handed her back to him. The fear and then the resignation. I know she isn't well but I can't get it out of my head. Hell, Mitch, maybe I'm making too much of this." But Zach's grip on his mug tightened almost as much as his gut did. Zach's gut had been screaming that he'd made a mistake since he'd returned Allison to Sandoval. And he'd learned to always go with his gut. It had saved his ass more times than he cared to count. He knew what he had to do. "Thanks for the coffee and the ear." He plopped the mug on the counter as he passed it on his way to the door.

"Zach?"

Zach glanced over his shoulder at Mitch.

"If you need anything ..." Mitch said.

The rest of that sentence wasn't necessary between them and Mitch left it unsaid. Zach nodded.

On his way out to his SUV, Zach called Chase. "Meet me at my place."

A short while later Chase joined Zach at the back of the house in the room Zach had designated as the command room for his organization. The room looked like a typical office with desks and computers. A couple of comfortable low-back couches backed against walls for the times Zach or his men pulled an all-nighter in here. A few rubber balls sat on the desk Chase favored to bounce against the tile floor or the wall when he was waiting on information.

Like the rest of Zach's place, the command room looked simple enough. To an outsider, the whole set up looked mild and gave no indication of the nature of his business which was exactly what Zach wanted.

Chase rubbed a hand over his trim goatee. "What's up?"

"We have an extraction."

"The rest of the team on the way?" Chase asked.

"No. It's going to be just you and me on this one."

"Okay. Who?"

"Allison Sandoval."

Chase's eyes narrowed. "The recovery you did this morning?"

"Yeah. We're taking her back. Sandoval is taking her home tonight. We need to get Allison out before then."

Zach could see a question in Chase's eyes and couldn't blame him. Zach had never turned around on a client. Doing so was a risk to his organization. Zach's business reputation was solid. His clients knew they could count on him. If he was wrong about this, his business would take a hit. No doubt Chase was thinking all that, but despite his questions and likely misgivings,

Chase nodded.

"How do you want to do this?" Chase asked.

"Get a blueprint for the hotel. When I asked you to check Sandoval out, you found out there's only one accommodation on that floor. The suite Sandoval is staying in."

Chase leaned back against a desk and crossed one ankle over the other. "He's staying there with his wife and three personal guards."

"With Sandoval himself, that makes only four men to get through."

"Easy enough," Chase agreed. "What's the plan?"

Zach eyed Chase. "They're going to take a nap."

* * *

Allison huddled on the floor of one of the bedrooms in the hotel suite. How long had she been in here? Hours? A day? She didn't know. She was no longer wearing the gown she'd had on for Rafael's gala. Where was her gown? She needed her gown. At the moment, she couldn't recall why the gown was all important, she just knew it was.

One of Rafael's guards had held her down while a second guard gave her an injection. The room was in darkness. At Rafael's order, the same guard who'd drugged her had removed all the light bulbs. Since her marriage to Rafael, Allison had learned to fear the dark. With her mind muddled, all kinds of horrors lived in the dark. She could see them now.

She drew her knees up tighter and pressed her brow hard against them. The images weren't real. *Not real.* The true stuff of nightmares weren't in this room with her, but elsewhere in this suite in the form of her husband. Over and over she told herself that, fighting the jumble in her mind. But how long could she fight it? Rafael hadn't given her enough of the drug today to push her over the edge into madness, but how long before he did? How much longer before she lost all touch with reality?

Her skin prickled with fear. She took a sharp breath and smelled smoke. She lifted her head from her knees. Was the smoke real or something else she was imagining? A sound came from the outer room, so faint she barely heard it, then light filled the room for an instant as her door was opened then closed. In that flash of light, something had filled the doorway and that something was now barreling toward her.

What was it? She couldn't make it out in the blackness. She cried out and shrank back, pressing her back hard against the wall.

A light came on. A flashlight held by a man who now stood over her. He was dressed casually in jeans and a jacket. He was big. She couldn't see his face. He wore some kind of mask. She wrapped her arms tight around herself.

The man crouched in front of her. "I've come to take you out of here."

In her drug induced state, his voice sounded like a recording being played at the wrong speed, too slow then too fast. Was the voice even real? Was the man real? She whimpered.

"It's all right. It's going to be all right," the man said. He was holding something. A face mask like the one he was wearing. "I want you to put this on." He turned his head and spoke into a device on his shoulder. "We're coming out."

Allison shook her head. "You're not real. You're not real!"

The man went still for an instant, then reached for her. Allison's eyelids fluttered and she lost consciousness.

* * *

Zach caught Allison before she hit the carpeting. He put the mask on her himself then removed his jacket and put that on her as well. It was cold out and he didn't have time to find a coat to put on her over the pants and thin blouse she wore. He swung her up into his arms and left the room. In the main area of the suite, Sandoval's guards were sprawled on couches, down for the count from the sleeping agent Chase had slid under the door. Sandoval wasn't with his guards. He was nowhere to be found in the suite which meant he could return at any moment.

Zach looked around, but Chase had retrieved the device that administered the sleeping agent. Chase was waiting by the door, should Sandoval make an untimely entrance. At Zach's appearance with Allison, Chase opened the outer door slowly, then nodded to Zach and led the way into the hall.

They walked by the elevator and entered the

stairwell. Zach waited, with Allison in his arms, while Chase removed Zach's mask and Allison's. Chase then removed his own mask and put them all in the duffel bag they'd left on the stair landing. Chase grabbed the bag and they began their descent down the stairs. Allison hadn't stirred when Chase removed her mask. She remained still in Zach's arms.

"She okay?" Chase asked.

Zach pressed his lips together, his expression grim. "She's spooked and she was exposed to the gas before I put the mask on her. That's all I know for sure. We'll have to see about the rest."

At the bottom of the stairwell, they took an exit that opened to the rear of the hotel. The building backed onto a quiet side street where Zach had parked his SUV.

A few moments later, he placed Allison carefully on the back seat and joined Chase in the front, taking his place behind the steering wheel.

Chase turned to Zach. "What next? Taking her back to your place?"

Zach started the engine, but cast a glance in his rearview mirror at Allison. She was asleep, but not relaxed. The skin on her brow was pulled taut from tension. Zach frowned, seeing it. "No."

* * *

Allison's eyes flew open. Her heart was pounding. Her breath was coming way too fast. Waking up in a panic wasn't a new thing. In the last months, she'd lived in constant fear.

"It's all right. You're okay."

She didn't know that voice. The room was dimly lit. A low bulb in a ceiling light fixture left the room in deep shadow. The male voice came out of the darkness. So dark. Her throat tightened.

The man who'd spoken moved into her range of vision and stood over her. She couldn't make him out clearly in the dull light but she had a flash of another man standing over her. In her hotel room. She gasped.

"No need to be afraid. You're okay."

"The light. Turn on the light!"

An instant later another ceiling light came on. Allison blinked at the brightness. This wasn't the man from her hotel room, if her foggy memory could be trusted. If that other man had been real. The man standing over her now had a shaggy mop of fair hair and brown eyes that crinkled at the corners with his smile. She felt another rush of panic. Was he real?

"Allison, can you hear me? You're all right," the man said.

That was still to be determined. "Where am I? Who are you?" She blurted out the words in a rush.

"My name is Brock St. John. I'm a doctor. You're at the clinic I operate with my wife, Laurel, who is also a doctor."

The injections Rafael gave Allison kept her desperately thirsty, caused excruciating headaches and left her trembling with fatigue. Her body felt heavy, weighted down, and her head pounded as if someone were chipping away at the inside with ice picks. She lifted her hand to her head, but was restrained by an IV line. "What are you giving me?" Her voice came out shrill. "Did Rafael bring me here?"

Allison fought back the bone-deep weariness and pushed herself up from the bed. She swung her legs over the side. She had to get out of here.

Brock cupped her shoulders. "Saline is in your IV. You're dehydrated. No, Rafael didn't bring you here."

The man—Brock—was looking down at her, concern in his eyes, and sincerity. While Brock didn't deny knowing who Rafael was, he didn't appear to be lying about Rafael bringing her here. Added to that, Brock's hold on her was gentle, keeping her upright but not restraining her. The knot in her stomach loosened just a little.

Allison stared up at him, not willing to trust him yet. "We've never met. How do you know me?"

Brock lowered his hands. "I don't know you. I know of you. You've been in the media, Allison. You were brought here yesterday for medical treatment."

Allison's heart thumped. "By whom? Who brought me?"

Another man appeared in the doorway, holding a steaming coffee mug. "I brought you here."

He entered the room. This man she recognized. He was the man Rafael had sent to return her to him—Zach. A low sound came from her throat and she shouted, "No!" She'd only thought she may have something to fear from Brock, but this man, the man who'd just entered the room, he'd already caused her harm. Terror gave her the adrenaline she needed to leap off the bed and onto the floor. She yanked at her IV line and shouted to the newcomer. "No! Don't come near me!"

Zach was making his way toward her, but stopped moving. He wore a short sleeve T-shirt and his biceps bulged against the tight material. On his right arm, just below the sleeve, he had a tattoo of the Navy Seal crest. Rafael's reach extended to the U.S. military. Allison's mouth went dry.

"Easy." Zach held her gaze. "I'll stay right here."

Brock's hand closed over hers, preventing her from yanking the IV out of her arm.

"Allison, it's okay. You're safe, I promise." Brock's words came quick and urgent.

Brock's concern seemed sincere. Had he been duped? Did he not know the other man worked for Rafael?

She stopped struggling against Brock's hold and stared up at him. "Listen to me. That man who just came in here? He is not to be trusted."

Brock released her and glanced over his shoulder at Zach who still stood in the middle of the room.

Zach held up the hand that wasn't holding the mug. "Allison, what Brock is telling you is true. You are safe here."

She refused to show him any more fear and instead lifted her chin and met him square in the eye. "You must take me for a fool. Do you think I've forgotten you work for Rafael?"

"I don't work for Sandoval. I don't work for anyone. I run a private organization. Sandoval came to me, telling me you were missing and that he needed help to find you."

Allison's insides quivered. "You did your job. Why am I here, or is this some sick game you and Rafael are playing?"

"I'm not into playing games. You're safe." Zach inclined his head once slowly, never taking his eyes from hers. "Believe it."

"It will take a lot more than your say-so to convince me what you're telling me now is the truth."

"Fair enough."

His agreement surprised her. She'd expected him to downplay or even dismiss her apprehension. She couldn't analyze his motives at this moment. Her pulse was racing. It was taking all she had to remain upright and the pain in her head hadn't let up.

Zach frowned. "I can see your headache in your eyes. Brock, what can you give her for that?"

Allison made a choking sound in her throat. "No. I don't want anything from you."

"Aspirin?" Zach said. "Brock, you must have that? In a new, sealed container."

Allison kept her gaze trained on Zach. Finally she looked to Brock and nodded.

"Be right back," Brock said.

She felt a moment of full-blown panic when Brock left her in the room alone with Zach. Silly, really, that she'd feel safer with the doctor present—as if Brock could help her protect herself against Zach. Brock wasn't close to matching

Zach in height, or, physically, anywhere else. The doctor had a lean, rangy build while the T-shirt Zach wore outlined a hard, chiseled body. Zach was a SEAL and obviously very skilled judging the way he'd taken her away from Rafael's trained guards.

Zach wore his light brown hair short. His blue eyes were serious and piercing, missing nothing, including, no doubt, her close scrutiny of him now.

He stood quiet under it, giving her the chance to take his measure. He'd said he wasn't into playing games, then what was he into? Why did he take her back from Rafael after returning her to him? The rush of adrenaline was wearing off and she desperately needed to sit down. She remained on her feet and kept her gaze fixed on his. "Why did you take me from the hotel?"

He gave her a level look. "I didn't know if you were safe where you were. I knew you'd be safe with me."

What had changed for him in the time he'd returned her to Rafael and now? She supposed she should be grateful that he'd changed his mind and got her away from Rafael, but it would be stupid and dangerous to trust this man.

Brock returned with the bottle of aspirin and a bottle of water and handed both to her. He'd kept his word. Both were sealed. Her hands trembled with the paltry effort of breaking the plastic wraps and twisting the caps off the bottles. She didn't want the two men to see how weak she was but she couldn't stop the shaking.

She drank deeply then took the pills. She

doubted any over-the-counter pain medicine would relieve this headache but she was desperate enough to take plain aspirin and hope, at least, it would take some of the edge off.

"Let me know if they don't do the trick," Brock said.

She focused on Brock. "It's not aspirin I need from you. I need to be away from here. Help me do that."

"You're safe. No one here is going to harm you," Brock said quietly. "I can't discharge you in your present condition. Give us some time to help you feel better and then leave."

Allison's mouth tightened with bitterness. Brock hadn't said he'd hold her against her will, but there'd be no help from him to get away from Zach.

"If you need anything more, let me know," Brock added. He nodded once to Zach then left the room.

She didn't have any intention of lingering here. First chance she got, she'd slip away, but how to get away? Where to go? The plan she'd devised that would ensure her safety from Rafael was no longer possible. What was she going to do now? She had no passport. No money. No transportation. Even now, Rafael could be on his way here. And when he got here ...

"Hey." Zach closed the distance between himself and Allison and grasped her shoulder. "Take a breath. You've lost all the color in your face."

"I really—" she closed her eyes, took a gulp of air "—have to get out of here. Prove you're as concerned about my safety as you claim. Don't stop me." But even as she said the words, she feared her ability to carry them out. The aftereffects of Rafael's injection and these last moments of being in fighting mode with Zach and Brock had depleted her. Not to mention the months prior that had sorely weakened her. She simply had nothing left in her.

But she had to try.

She opened her eyes and took a step away from the bed. Her head swam. Zach plopped his coffee onto a nightstand and grabbed her, preventing her from hitting the floor with her face.

His eyes narrowed in that penetrating gaze she'd seen from him before. "You're not in any condition to go anywhere. Let Brock do his thing. Get you feeling better then we'll talk about where you go next."

Her eyelids fluttered and she fought to keep them open. "I don't trust you." With her last burst of strength, she pushed back at Zach, but it was like a lamb striking out at a lion.

Whatever he said next, if he responded at all, Allison didn't hear him.

CHAPTER FOUR

Allison sagged against him. Her breathing was deep and even in sleep. She was exhausted. Zach lifted her into his arms and set her gently onto the bed.

Her fear got to him. She was afraid of him. Afraid because she believed he worked for Sandoval. Sandoval claimed she was mentally unstable. If so, it made sense that her fear of him was the product of her damaged mind. But something felt off. Zach hadn't changed his mind about that.

These moments with her had only reinforced his doubts and Zach wanted answers about her condition now. He was tense from the not knowing. He made sure none of that tension was in his touch and reached out, gently raising the covers over her, then left the room to find Brock.

It was just seven a.m. Brock and Laurel kept a small staff and a shift change was underway as the night nurses were replaced by the day. Zach passed the women on their way out as he prowled the clinic in search of Brock.

Brock was in the kitchen pouring coffee into a chipped blue mug. Like Zach, he'd been up all night. He looked up, his eyes showing the strain of the night without sleep, as Zach charged into the room.

Brock stopped mid-pour. "I made a fresh pot. Want some?"

Zach ignored the question and asked his own. "Did you get the tox screen back on Allison?"

"Yeah, I put a rush on it. It came while you were in with her." Brock finished filling his mug. "Results on medications for the type of illness you described were negative."

Zach eyed Brock. "Those meds would show up on a tox."

"Yeah, they would." Brock added cream to his mug then stirred. "Given what you told me about her condition when you found her, and what I witnessed when you brought her in, I expanded the search."

Zach went still. "And?"

Brock's lips firmed. "One hit. Not for the kind of drug to combat hallucinations and delusions. It's the kind that causes them." He tossed the spoon into the sink in an outward display of the anger he was obviously feeling.

Zach's gut clenched. "You sure?"

"No doubt and the marks on her skin show she's received injections regularly."

She'd been wearing a dress with sleeves when Zach found her in the alley and then a long-sleeved blouse in her hotel room. He hadn't seen any track marks.

"Someone's been inducing Allison's hallucinations. A husband should have seen marks on his wife—marks that appeared at the same time as her hallucinations," Brock added pointedly.

"Sandoval?" Zach's mouth tightened. "She's terrified of him."

"This could be the reason. She should be able to shed some light on all this."

"I plan on asking her." Why would Sandoval drug his wife? Zach let that question go for his more immediate concern. "How bad is she?"

"She'll go through a period of withdrawal over the next seventy-two to ninety-six hours. The drug will take time to work its way out of her system." Brock's concern was obvious in his tone. "On the plus side, once she's drug free there won't be lingering effects that go on for months. No concern that the drug will remain dormant in her system for years until something triggers it. She's underweight, undernourished. Her immune system is down. I started a course of antibiotics to fight off infection."

Zach felt a surge of anger at her condition. "What the hell."

"Yeah," Brock said somberly. "I'll see her myself and explain all of this to her. I'm not well equipped to handle withdrawal here. She should spend some time in rehab though I'm getting that's not a good idea, that you want to keep her out of sight."

"Yeah. Do what you can for her here, Brock. We need to keep her off the grid for the time being."

"I got that. There's more," Brock said quietly. "While she was under I did a thorough exam. She's been beaten. I found marks on her abdomen. Her back. By the locations I'd say the bastard who did this kept to parts of her body that would be covered by clothing."

Zach's jaw tightened. He was getting more enraged by the minute.

Brock blew out a breath. "Zach, I'm getting that this woman means something to you."

"It's not like that. Allison is a job that felt wrong. I don't have all the answers yet, but I've had a bad feeling from the start of it that I called this wrong."

It was looking like he'd called it wrong big time. He felt a responsibility to Allison over that. He ran a hand back through his hair and without another word to Brock went back to Allison's room. She was still sleeping. He rubbed a hand down his face and dropped into the chair at her bedside.

Allison's eyes flew open and her body began to thrash on the bed. Zach shot to his feet and put his hands on her arms to keep her from falling off the mattress. "Allison, you're all right."

"Go away! Go away!" Allison made a soft, mewling sound. "Make it go away!"

"Brock!" Zach shouted. "Get in here!"

Allison screamed, a sound of terror that tightened Zach's stomach. He lifted her into his arms and pressed her against his chest so she couldn't do herself any harm with her wild movement. She was trembling in his arms.

"Allison, you're all right. You're okay. It's not real. A hallucination. Not real."

Brock ran in. He had a small bottle in one hand and while he sprinted to the IV, he filled a syringe with whatever was in that bottle. As soon as he reached the IV bag, he added the medication.

Allison's teeth chattered. She was cold now. Zach could feel the drop in her body temperature. Keeping one arm locked around her, he used his free hand to rub up and down her back and stimulate circulation. He recalled what Brock had said, that she'd been beaten there, and softened his touch. "Brock, how long for that stuff to work?"

Zach had barely shouted the words when Allison drooped against him. Carefully, he set her back on the bed. He stepped back for Brock to take his place at Allison's bedside. She was out of it. Her eyes closed. Her body still. She was unaware of Brock as he spent the next few minutes checking her vitals.

"She'll be out of it for a while," Brock said quietly.

And when she woke, would she go through that all over again? Zach had seen a lot, but this struck him.

He was out of his depth here. This was Brock's gig, not his. Zach needed to get himself back on solid ground.

"We've both been up all night." Brock rubbed his eyes. "I still have rounds. You're welcome to use the couch in my office to crash."

"In a bit."

As Brock left, Zach unclipped his cell phone and moved away from the bed. He called Chase, keeping his voice low not to disturb Allison.

"Zach?" Chase said.

"What's the word on yesterday?"

"Sandoval hasn't left the country yet. He must be looking for his wife but no one's come here calling. I figure no reason he should unless he wants to hire us to find her a second time."

"Yeah. By now he'd have to figure by the smooth in and out this was a pro job. Sandoval's father made a lot of enemies." Zach grunted. "Rafael Sandoval could spend his lifetime going through the list of people who could have snatched Allison to get back at him. Chase, you mentioned Allison has family. Parents and one sister. Put a couple of our people on them. I want our men to report back to me if Sandoval shows up there looking for Allison and to provide protection should her family need it from him."

"Consider it done. How is she?" Chase asked.

Zach frowned and his gaze went to her. "Not good."

There was a brief silence then Chase said, "Roger Morse called."

Morse had referred Sandoval. "What does he want?"

"Wouldn't say. Only that he wants to meet with you."

Morse was CIA. Zach's organization did a lot of off-the-books work for Morse. Zach didn't like Morse. Trusted him less. That was enough reason not to blow off a meeting. "I'll set it up with him. Anything else?"

"That's all of it," Chase said.

Zach ended the call and placed another, this time to Morse. Morse answered on the first ring. "It's Corrigan."

"I need to see you."

"What about?"

"Let's talk in person. Your place."

Morse's voice was tense, strained. Zach glanced at his watch. "Noon."

"I'll be there."

Zach disconnected. Morse was a tense son of a bitch by nature, but even for him this was too tense. What the hell was up?

Zach called Chase back. "I need you to do something for me. I need to leave Brock's to meet Morse. I need you to come here and watch Allison. I don't want her taken out of here. No one gets near her, Chase."

"Understood," Chase said.

Zach ended the call. He wanted to speak with Allison before he left to meet Morse and tell her about Chase. She'd be out a while longer from what Brock gave her. Brock's couch sounded good. Zach would welcome some sleep. But he wouldn't be making use of it. He glanced at Allison. She'd been drugged and beaten. He wasn't going to leave her alone and unprotected. Instead of heading to Brock's office, Zach returned to the chair at her bedside.

* * *

Allison opened her eyes and remembered the images, the creatures. She looked wildly about her. They were gone.

Zach sat in the chair by her bed. Her first reaction was fear—he worked for Rafael—but Zach was alone. So far he hadn't called Rafael. If he had, she'd be having a very different awakening.

His eyes were open and on her. He leaned forward in the chair. His brows pulled together. "How you feeling?"

He'd been present when she'd had her meltdown. She recalled seeing him in all the chaos of her mind. Recalled him taking her into his arms. She crossed her own arms, gripping her elbows. She was afraid of him and his connection to Rafael. She was embarrassed and ashamed. She closed her eyes at the sting of tears. Dammit she was not going to lose it again. She lowered her gaze, blinking quickly, and kept her eyes down until she was sure she wouldn't break down. When she glanced up again, Zach's eyes were still on her. "I didn't expect you to still be here."

"Where did you expect me to be?" he asked mildly.

"Back where you come from doing whatever it is you do."

"Not yet. You haven't answered me. How are you feeling?"

Shaky. Terrified. Like she was losing her grip on her sanity. She increased her grip on her elbows until she could feel the skin stretch tight across her knuckles. "I'm not insane." She blurted out the words, words she'd been telling herself for the last months, all the while praying they were true.

Zach's gaze held hers and his deep voice grew

gentle as he said, "I know that. Brock found a drug in your system that causes the kinds of things you've been experiencing."

He could never know how much hearing those words meant to her. Someone else knew about the injections. She closed her eyes, overcome for a moment. But it was a brief moment. Zach worked for Rafael. Of course he knew all about the drugs.

"You need to get better," Zach said. "You need to kick this."

He was treating her like an addict. She wanted to protest but couldn't. Was she addicted to Rafael's drug? Her throat clogged and again she had to fight back tears.

"Brock was going to recommend a rehab facility for you," Zach went on.

Rehab? She studied him. Was he telling her the truth? Or was rehab his way of getting her to go quietly back to Rafael? She didn't trust Zach—not after he'd returned her to Rafael—and she still didn't know what his motives were for taking her out of Rafael's hotel room. She wanted nothing more than to end the feelings Rafael's drug induced, but if Zach was being truthful about rehab, she couldn't remain in one place long enough to get help to do that. She couldn't go to a rehab facility. Rafael would find her if she didn't keep moving.

Zach's mouth thinned. "I've asked Brock to hold off and treat you here instead where we can keep you hidden."

As in hidden from Rafael? Why would Zach care about that?

"Allison." Zach leaned in closer to her. "Who's been giving you that drug?"

His voice was low and urgent. His question angered her and her cheeks heated. "Do you expect me to believe you don't know that?"

He didn't flinch. His gaze remained steady. "Who?"

Allison twisted her lips bitterly. "Do you honestly think I believe you don't know that the man you work for—my husband—has been drugging me?" She tasted bile that Rafael was her husband.

Zach's expression became fierce. "Why?"

She couldn't imagine why he was outraged. "Why do you think?"

"I'm asking."

"Why don't you ask your boss?" She held up a hand. "Oh, that's right. You don't work for Rafael." Her tone was sarcastic. Zach didn't respond, just continued to regard her with that unwavering stare. She'd said too much already. Her insides tightened. She stopped speaking and swallowed convulsively for a moment.

"Allison?" When she remained silent, he blew out an impatient breath. "I have to leave for a while. I'll be back later today. We'll pick this up then." Zach stopped speaking then said gently, "I'm not a mind reader. Tell me what you're thinking."

No, she wouldn't do that. Before she could tell him so, a woman entered the room, bearing a tray.

"Here's breakfast for you, Allison." The woman smiled and deep lines cut into her ruddy cheeks. "Zach, I can bring some for you too."

"Thanks, Mary, but I'm on my way out."

He got to his feet and Mary set a covered tray on the small table at Allison's bedside.

"Let me know if you change your mind and you want to eat before you go," Mary said to Zach.

"Appreciate it. Thank you."

"Allison, you must be feeling hungry. Let me set this up for you," Mary said.

Mary uncovered the tray revealing a plate of toast and eggs, a mug of coffee, and a tall glass of juice. Allison's mouth watered. It had been so long since she'd had real food. She'd lost weight in the last months. Her ribs and bones protruded. She looked like a scarecrow. It was all she could do now not to pounce on the tray. She curled her fingers into her palms to keep from doing that. She couldn't trust this food. She didn't know if it had been drugged.

Allison expected Zach to leave her with the other woman, but he remained by the bed. Mary was the one to leave.

Zach addressed Allison. "While I'm gone, one of my people will stay here with you. His name is Gavin Chase."

Alarm tightened Allison's stomach. "If you're not working for Rafael, why are you leaving a man to keep me a prisoner here?"

Zach shook his head once slowly. "Not to imprison you. To protect you. Chase won't let anyone who hasn't been cleared by Brock near you." Zach's jaw clenched. "Including Sandoval."

There was no way to misinterpret Zach's anger

when he'd said Rafael's name. Why was he putting on this act?

"Chase," Zach called out and a man entered her room. "Allison, this is Gavin Chase."

Chase was tall and muscled with a trim goatee that suited him well.

"Allison," Chase said in acknowledgment. He smiled. "I'll be out in the hall if you need me."

As Chase left the room, Zach said to her, "I'll see you later." He turned away from her.

"Wait."

He turned back to face her.

"If you're really not working for Rafael," Allison's tone was laced with bitterness, "why are you still here with me? Why not just leave me?"

He frowned and she could tell he had no liking for the question. Still, his gaze was direct as he responded. "I called this wrong with you and Sandoval and you were hurt because of it. I don't know where you were going when you left him, but I shouldn't have stopped you."

Allison watched him leave the room. He sounded sincere. He looked sincere. But she didn't believe him. She was so desperate to have someone in her life she could trust again. She hated being on her guard all the time, afraid to believe in anyone. Taking people at their word was a luxury she hadn't had in a long time. She'd done that with Rafael. She wouldn't make that mistake again. This time a mistake would not affect only her. So many other lives were at stake. She didn't know how she'd be able to save them now that all she'd planned had been lost, but she had to find a way.

The steam rising off the tray Mary had left filled the room with the various food smells. Hospital food was reputed to be among the worst, but this food smelled like the finest five star cuisine to Allison. Her hands shook as she put the cover back on the tray in an attempt to block out some of the aroma.

" ... Sandoval."

Zach's voice came from the hall. Allison's head came up sharply. Though Zach was speaking quietly, the door was open. Was Rafael on his way here? Her heart picked up its pace. She strained her ears but couldn't make out anymore of what Zach was saying. Careful not to make any sound that would alert Zach and Chase that she'd ventured closer, she made her way to the wall behind the door and leaned against it.

" ... it's likely Morse wants to know about your meeting with Sandoval," Chase said.

"Yeah."

Zach again.

"No doubt he had a reason for referring Sandoval to you," Chase added. "Morse never does anything without a reason that benefits him. And if he knows we have Allison, and that Sandoval is looking for his wife, I'm betting he's going to want you to give her to him. She would be a valuable card to play with Sandoval." Chase paused. "Zach, we do a lot of business for Morse and the CIA."

A chill went through Allison.

"Hi Zach. Chase."

Allison recognized Mary's voice.

"Hey Mary," Chase said. "What you got

there?"

"Just going to check Allison's vitals again."

Allison made it back to the bed as Mary breezed into her room. That minor exertion had left Allison panting and she worked to regulate her breathing.

Mary came to Allison's bedside and attached a blood pressure cuff. "Dr. St. John wants another reading." She smiled.

Allison's heart was beating hard. Zach intended to hand her over to the CIA who would then return her to Rafael. She couldn't let that happen.

Mary frowned. "Your BP's up. I know being in a hospital can be stressful but try to relax, hon. The sooner you get better, the sooner you can go home." Mary uncovered the food tray again then said with a smile, "Eat up before it gets cold."

When Mary reached the hall, Allison heard her tell Chase where he could get breakfast. They exchanged another few words then the conversation ended. Mary had only addressed Chase. Zach must have left for his meeting with the CIA.

Allison needed to be away from here. Out from under Zach's "so called" protection. She didn't believe Chase would leave his post for breakfast. How long did she have before he checked in on her? She couldn't afford to waste any time.

She found her clothing neatly hung in the small closet. She dressed in the black pants and white cotton shirt she'd had on in the hotel room. There was a man's jacket in the closet as well. Zach had placed one of his around her at the alley. This wasn't that one, but it was just as large. She didn't know what it was doing here, but was glad for it.

She didn't have the gown she was wearing the night she'd escaped from Rafael. That gown would have guaranteed her safety from him. The dress was lost. She had to move on without it.

This clinic was unlike any other hospital facility she'd ever been in. It was fashioned more like a dwelling, a single story house. If not for the medical equipment, her room resembled a typical bedroom. And like all bedrooms, this one had windows.

CHAPTER FIVE

Zach was still thinking about what Allison had told him about Sandoval. The look in her eyes when she'd named Sandoval as the one who'd given her the drugs had been haunted and anguished. Along with that pain there'd been terror. She was scared out of her head of Sandoval. No wonder. Zach's grip on the steering wheel tightened.

Sandoval had lied to Zach and that lie resulted in a woman being hurt. She'd been drugged and beaten. The fact that Zach had played a part in enabling Sandoval to hurt Allison turned his stomach.

He shouldn't have stopped her from getting away from Sandoval. He blew out a breath filled with regret. There was no way he could fully make that right, undo the hurt Sandoval had inflicted on her. But Zach could and would escort Allison to wherever she'd been headed before he'd intervened.

The road leading directly to Zach's place came into view. Zach made the turn, not surprised to find Morse waiting by the road side, engine idling. Zach followed the road to its end then parked at the back of the house. He entered the security code for the command room then went inside, not waiting for Morse to park his own vehicle. Zach left the door open. Morse hurried in almost on Zach's heels.

Zach crossed his arms and without preamble asked, "What's going on Morse?"

Roger Morse was in his mid fifties, stocky, with graying curly hair that was thinning on top. He ran a finger that was stained yellow from tobacco over an almost bald patch. "What happened with Sandoval?"

"What do you mean?"

"Cut the shit, Zach. Tell me what Sandoval wanted to talk to you about so badly."

"You got something going on with Sandoval?"

"Fuck, Zach, you're a closemouthed son of a bitch."

"That works for you, Morse. I do a lot for you that can't be said. Now what's going on with Sandoval?"

Morse's expression tightened. "I didn't come here to give information. I came to get it."

Zach kept his eyes on Morse and kept his silence. Morse wanted to be in control. Zach did jobs for Morse, but Morse didn't run him and Zach had made sure Morse knew that. There was no love lost between them and Zach knew Morse would rather not work with him at all, but he did because Zach and his people were that good.

Morse clenched his jaw tight enough that it bulged. "I need to know if Sandoval hired you. If something's going down in his country."

Zach knew the history. Rafael Sandoval's father, Enrique, had a choke-hold on the region, getting rid of any opposition fast and hard. Since the demise of the dictator, the rebels wanting to overthrow the Sandoval regime had resurfaced.

"Sandoval says he wants to end the old ways," Morse went on. "To democratize his country. He's looking to the U.S. for funds. He needs to show the world he's able to lead his country. Did he hire you to restore order?"

Zach couldn't say he'd never done what Morse was asking. There were always two sides to every conflict. But Zach had always decided for himself which side he would support, which missions to accept. He'd never let anything or anyone decide that for him. And the deciding factor was always if he felt the mission was just. He had to feel the rightness of it. He wasn't going to bare his soul to Morse. To Morse now, Zach said simply, "Sandoval doesn't need me and my people. He's got his own army."

"With the world watching him right now, he's not going to want to remove this threat himself. It'll be better politically to have someone from outside quietly do his work for him." Morse kept his gaze trained on Zach. "If that's not it, I can't think of any other reason he'd need to talk to you. Give me something, here, Zach."

Zach eyed Morse. "He didn't come to me to do clean up. If you suspect that's what he's doing, he's hired out elsewhere."

Morse rubbed the top of his head. "Shit. I was hoping you were on your way down there at Rafael's request."

"Why's that?"

Morse looked rattled. "It would be the perfect cover to do the reconnaissance I need."

"Why do you need recon there?"

Morse shook his head. "No matter now since you're not on Sandoval's payroll. Let me know if that changes. I'll have a job for you." Morse was silent for a moment then said, "There is something you can do. Sandoval's talks here are finished for the time being, but he's still hanging around. He's keeping this under wraps, but we found out his wife took off. She was here with him on his diplomatic visit and now she's gone. His people are quietly looking for her. No Intel on why she left him, but the fact that she did leave could help us."

"How?"

"She's been with Sandoval for several months. She may know something we can use."

"Like what?" When Morse didn't respond, Zach prodded. "Big 'if', Morse. For all you know, she may have taken off because she's rethinking her marriage."

"Could be," Morse said but Zach could see in Morse's eyes he didn't believe that. Morse shrugged though he looked anything but indifferent. "Find Allison Sandoval."

Morse knew something about Allison and the fact that he did made Zach uneasy. "Who've you got looking for her now? Your people or did you bring in outside help?"

"No one."

Zach didn't believe that. His voice hard he said, "All the best finding her, Morse."

Morse pressed his lips together. "I could use your help with this. Are you in?"

"You ready to be straight with me about what's really going on here?"

Morse's face reddened and he remained silent.

Zach gave Morse a look that was now as hard as his tone. "Like I said, all the best finding her."

Morse turned away from Zach and without a word left the command room, slamming the door behind him. Chase had been right about Morse wanting Allison. Morse wanted her badly. Morse was an asshole but he was good at his job. If he believed Allison had information about Sandoval, Zach couldn't discount the possibility.

Zach's cell phone rang. "Go ahead, Chase."

"We got a problem. Allison left Brock's."

"What?"

"Yeah." Chase emitted a harsh breath of frustration. "She went out the window in her room. I took a look directly around the clinic and didn't find her. There's a lot of woods to cover and it gets dark early now. I want to call in Briggs and Hamilton to help."

It would take his men some time to get to Brock's. Just as it would take Zach. As long as she was out there alone, without his protection, she was vulnerable. Acid burned Zach's stomach. They had to find her. "Get on it, Chase. I'm on my way."

* * *

Brock's clinic was indeed a house and in a rural part of New York, Allison realized as she made her way from it. She'd been unconscious when Zach had brought her here and unable to get her bearings. Now she saw there was only one road leading to and from the clinic with bush and forests on both sides.

The air smelled of damp earth and some wild floral scent Allison couldn't identify. She kept to the trees as much as possible. The last thing she wanted was to be seen by an oncoming car. That didn't prove to be a concern, though, as time passed and she had yet to see even one vehicle on this road.

The day was overcast and bitterly cold. She was glad of the jacket she wore that was warm and so huge it hung past her knees and over her hands. Clouds looked heavy with the promise of snow.

She hadn't come across another person since leaving Brock's. As she walked on, the feeling of isolation, of being alone in the world grew. She savored it, feeling safer than she had in a long time. She shook her head. It was a false sense of security, one she couldn't indulge in.

She wished she could have trusted her safety at Brock's and stayed there a while longer to regain the strength that the last months had depleted. Of course she couldn't. Not only did she need to keep moving, but she didn't trust Zach. For all she knew, he could have taken her from Rafael in an attempt to build her trust. To find out for Rafael all she knew about him and what, if anything, she'd done with that knowledge.

She hadn't done anything with that knowledge. She'd had proof of what she knew. Now she didn't. Without that proof, who would believe her? Rafael had planted the seeds of her mental illness so she wouldn't be believed. There were times she doubted her own sanity.

She could not remain in New York where Rafael had last known her to be. If she stayed here, it would only be a short time before he found her. She had to get away from here. That required money. All she had was what she was wearing. The man's jacket looked expensive. It was warm. She didn't want to part with it. Added to that, it wasn't hers. She swallowed hard, feeling like a thief. But there was no choice. Survival obviously came first. She'd pawn it for one that was less costly, and any additional money it might bring, at the first place she could.

Her strength was fading fast and worse than that, she was beginning to feel another bout of withdrawal. Her mouth tightened in frustration at her weakness. She had to control it and put one foot in front of the other and move on.

The temperature was dropping quickly. She could feel it. The sky had grown dark. A storm appeared to be imminent. The trees overhead let in little of the remaining light to filter through the branches. She needed to find a place to stay out of whatever weather was coming but it was dangerous to stop moving. Now not only did she have Rafael to worry about finding her, but Zach and his watchdog, Chase, as well.

Zach would have no reason to look for her if he weren't working for Rafael. Yes, he'd sounded sincere earlier when he'd said he shouldn't have interfered in her escape from Rafael. Those words could have her thinking he meant to set things right. That he was an honorable man. She wasn't that big a fool. Not anymore. Marriage to Rafael had cured her of that. If she'd thought she was being unfair to Zach, painting him with the same brush as Rafael, Zach himself had shown her he was no different from her husband. Barely moments after delivering that speech about protecting her, Zach went to meet with the CIA to hand her over. The thought was bitter. It gave her no satisfaction to be right. She wished Zach could have been the man he'd claimed to be.

She hated that along with the regret of finding out the truth about him, she also felt sadness. It scared her how much she wanted to believe in someone and how let down she now felt.

She was so tired. It was becoming a monumental effort to keep moving. Despite the frigid air, perspiration broke out on the back of her neck. Her heart rate accelerated. She could feel the withdrawal taking hold. Fight it. *Fight it.* A pain in her stomach halted her in her tracks and doubled her over.

She sucked in her breath and remained still, hoping to ride it out, but there was no riding it out. The pain sharpened. She squeezed her eyes shut and clutched her middle. Pressing her lips tightly together she fought to keep from crying out at the pain.

Tremors shook her. She reached out to steady herself against a tree trunk but stumbled. Her legs gave out and she landed hard on the cold ground.

Pain knifed through her. The tree no longer appeared a shelter, but a menacing beast looming over her, the branches, the tentacles, reaching out to envelope her. Allison screamed.

* * *

Zach, Chase, Hamilton and Briggs had been combing the area leading from Brock's for a while. The wind had kicked up causing the trees to sway. Zach narrowed his eyes against the sting of the cold breeze and entered a section of the woods where the trees and shrubs were less dense.

Where was she? She was skittish of strangers and even if a car happened along, it was unlikely she rode her thumb off this road. No, she wouldn't hitch. On foot, she couldn't have gone far. She had to still be in the area.

He didn't think she'd been taken by Sandoval or Morse. Zach and his people had moved quickly as soon as Chase discovered her gone and Zach had not had any indicators that Sandoval or Morse were close. Still, the possibility existed. Zach's shoulders were tense and his stomach hadn't eased since he'd received Chase's call.

The mic on Zach's shoulder remained quiet. One of his team would have reported in if they'd found her. His steps thudding on the hard, dry ground, and the whistle of the wind were the only sounds.

He walked on. He glanced at the sky. Clouds hung low, making the day darker, but there were still a few hours of daylight left. Zach didn't want to think they'd still be searching for her when night fell. He picked up his pace.

A woman screamed. He stopped on a trail. He swung in the direction of the sound then broke into a run.

A clearing was up ahead. He charged into it. Allison was huddled in a ball beneath a tree.

Zach dropped to his knees beside her. "Allison!"

She didn't respond. Was she even aware of his presence? Her eyes were wide, the pupils hugely dilated. She was trembling. He reached out to gently brush a leaf from her face. Her skin was pale, cold, and damp with perspiration.

She hadn't reacted to him at all but when the backs of his fingers touched her cheek, she screamed again and struggled to scoot back from him. She wasn't successful at putting any more distance between them.

"Not real. Not real."

Her tone was barely a whisper as if she lacked the strength to speak louder. The agony in her voice staggered him. "Allison. I'm going to help you."

Tears filled her eyes and streamed down her cheeks. Her gaze became fixed, locked on something within her mind.

Zach spoke into the mic. "I have her. I'm going to carry her north to Brock's. Chase, we'll make better time getting her help if you meet me on the road with one of our vehicles."

"On my way," Chase said.

Zach gently lifted Allison into his arms. He'd expected resistance but she was inert and unresponsive. A chill went through him. He tightened his grip on her and huddled over her to shield her from the wind and cold. "Hold on, Allison." He placed his lips to her ear and repeated, "Hold on."

CHAPTER SIX

Allison opened her eyes. Zach shot forward in the chair by her bedside but no, her gaze was clear, focused, and minus that all-consuming fear that had been present for the last three days when she'd been in the grip of withdrawal and seeing all manner of horrors. Zach exhaled what felt like his first deep breath in that time.

"Hey," he said.

She squinted at him then turned her head, looking around her. "I'm back at the clinic?"

Her voice was hoarse and he hated to see the fear back in her eyes. "Yeah. I found you out of it in the woods near here and brought you back."

She swallowed. "How long ago?"

"Three days."

She put her hand to her head. "So much time. I don't remember." She pressed her palms to the bed. Her arms trembled as she struggled to push herself up from her prone position on the mattress. "Rafael could have found me. He could have ... "

Her breathing quickened and she paled. Her pallor alarmed him and Zach grasped her shoulders. They were trembling like the rest of her. He squeezed gently. "None of that happened. You're here. You're safe. You're okay."

She drew back from him as far as she could with him still holding her. "Until the CIA arrives."

"What?"

"I overheard you and Chase. You were on your way to a meeting with the CIA. To hand me over."

On top of everything else, his conversation with Chase had added to her fear. She was still pulling against his hold. The desire to put distance from him was in her eyes if Zach hadn't received the message from her tugging, but he continued to hold her. "You got that wrong," Zach said gently. "Yes, I was meeting with my CIA contact, but not to give you to him. I was gathering information. That's all."

She raised her chin, though it trembled. "You must think I'm the world's biggest idiot. You do a lot of work for the CIA. I heard Chase say that. They scratch your back. You scratch theirs."

There was bitterness and sadness in her voice. He was sorry she believed him to be the one to cause her to feel them. Zach's manner softened further. "That's not how I roll. And, if you need proof, you're still here and not at a CIA facility."

"Allison, you're awake," Brock said with a broad smile as he made his way into her room and to her bedside. "Let's have a look at you. Hey,

Zach."

Zach shot Brock a look, displeased with the interruption. He let out a breath, acknowledging it was a necessary interruption. He needed to speak with Allison but that wasn't happening anyway. She was as closed off to him as she'd been when they'd first met. Any headway he'd made with her in getting her to trust him, if he'd made any, had been lost when she'd overheard his conversation about Morse. He was back to square one.

He rose from the chair to give Brock and Allison privacy for the examination. Out in the hall, Zach rubbed a hand over his jaw that was badly in need of a shave and fought back the fatigue of the last three days. Brock had explained he wasn't set up to treat Allison. Brock didn't have the staff so Zach had taken turns with Brock, Laurel, and their nurses, staying with Allison while she'd battled withdrawal. Seeing her that way, fighting a war within her own body, had affected him. Anger boiled him at her condition and he felt a helplessness he wasn't used to. He rolled one shoulder, feeling restless and out of sorts.

He needed to check in with Chase for an update on Sandoval and now, Morse, as well. He did that and Chase reported no change on their end. So far, no one had placed Allison with Zach. He ended the call with Chase.

Sandoval had a man hunt going for her. She was hiding something. Something Zach would bet was the reason Sandoval was so hot to find her. Zach snorted. It certainly wasn't husbandly devotion. Whatever was going on with her and Sandoval had Morse's antennae up as well.

Zach's first priority was protecting her. Whatever she believed to the contrary. His lips twisted sourly. While he understood her fear, he was frustrated with the situation and his inability to get through to her. He needed to find out what she was hiding, but she wasn't going to come clean with him now. He hated like hell flying blind. He needed to know what she knew and he needed to know what Morse was holding back. Again, Zach rolled his tense shoulders. While he had no choice with Allison at the moment, he knew where he could get the information Morse was sitting on.

Zach punched in the numbers for Gage's cell. Gage Broderick was a police captain in a D.C. precinct. As the phone was ringing, Zach realized it was six a.m. here in New York—three a.m. outside of Washington where Gage was. Zach was about to disconnect and call back at a more reasonable hour, when Gage's voice, heavy with sleep, came on the line.

"Zach?"

"Yeah. No one died."

Gage cleared his hoarse voice. "Glad to hear it."

Zach heard the mattress shift as Gage moved, then the sleepy voice of Mallory, Gage's fiancée. Zach winced. Shit. Gage had said Mallory wasn't sleeping well. Zach hated like hell that he'd awakened her.

"Is everything all right with Zach?" Mallory asked.

"All's good." Zach heard Gage kiss her. "Go back to sleep, honey."

Gage was quiet, his footfalls the only sounds for a moment, then a chair creaked and Zach figured Gage was now seated behind his desk in the spare room in his house that he used for a home office.

"Back now," Gage said.

"Sorry for the hour, man. Apologize to Mallory for me. How's she doing?"

"Some days are better than others."

Mallory had nearly died in the investigation that had brought her and Gage together. She'd been fighting that trauma since. Zach heard the worry in Gage's voice and shared it.

"She's been through a lot," Zach said.

"Yeah." Gage blew out a breath that conveyed his anxiety and helplessness, then asked, "What's going on with you, Zach? You okay?"

Zach figured Gage didn't need anything more on his plate at the moment and said simply, "I need a favor."

"Name it."

"I need a number for John." John was John Burke, Mallory's brother. Zach knew John and his wife, Eve, through Gage and Mallory and counted them as family. Mallory's brother was a CIA operative. John headed up a team of agents who specialized in chemical weapons terrorism. His advanced position with the CIA gave him a high level of clearance. If anyone could find out what Morse had declined to tell Zach, John could. Zach had the numbers for John's personal lines and that wasn't what he was after. "I need the number for his secure line, Gage."

Gage was still, then his chair squeaked again. "I was wondering why you were calling me from your secure line." Gage recited John's number.

"Got it," Zach said.

Gage's voice grew heavy with concern. "If you need to talk to John on that phone, you're into some heavy shit. Watch your ass."

"Guaranteed."

"See you in three weeks."

Thanksgiving was in a little over three weeks' time. Ed and Ellen Turner, Mitch's folks, and the people Zach thought of as his folks as well, always celebrated the day with their family and those fortunate to be considered family like Zach. Zach could count on one hand the times he'd missed Thanksgiving with the Turners since he was a boy. If he wasn't out of the country on a mission, he was there. "Yeah. Three weeks."

Zach ended the call. John lived in Virginia, near the CIA headquarters. Virginia was in the same time zone. Zach placed the call but got John's voicemail. He left a message for John to call him back on Zach's own secure line and left the number.

Zach returned to Allison's room. The door was open. Brock had left. Zach lingered in the doorway. She hadn't noticed him yet standing there. She didn't look up to answering the questions he needed to ask her and he felt like an ogre. She looked frightened and fragile. Allison didn't want his help but she needed it, and though it would be a hell of a lot easier, he couldn't turn his back on her.

But in order for him to protect her, he needed to know just what she was mixed up in. It all came back to that. He didn't know all he should. He had to take another stab at getting her to come clean with him.

He entered her room. Allison's head darted up.

"We need to talk," he said.

Allison's posture stiffened and her eyes became wary.

Zach sat in the usual chair. "I need to know why Sandoval is so hot to find you." She looked away from him, but not before he saw a veil come over her eyes, shielding them from him. "Allison, the time for secrets is over," he said gently. "I already told you I met with my CIA contact to gather information. What I found out was the CIA is hot for you too. Why is that?"

She continued to meet his gaze, her own now defiant. "You've been talking to the CIA. You tell me."

His anger sparked but died quickly. Despite the tough front, her voice was thin and weak. Her face pale and drawn. The ordeal of the last few days had ravaged her. And on top of that, she looked scared. He hated the fear in her eyes. She'd had too much of it.

Zach saw all that and wasn't immune to it. He blew out a breath. He had to tamp down on those thoughts. They would have him putting off questioning her. He had to press on. This was too important for him not to. "I know you had no reason to trust me but that was before. I got you away from Sandoval."

Her chin lifted. "How do I know that wasn't a

ruse to draw me in and you aren't on a fishing expedition for him?"

Zach's tone low and even, he said, "Do you see Sandoval here? I've hidden you from him. Do you see the CIA here? Do you honestly think if either of them knew you were here, they wouldn't be?"

Her gaze lowered but not before he saw in her eyes that she agreed with that.

"I've hidden you from Sandoval and now from the CIA as well. Got you treatment that you badly needed. While you were out of it, I could have given you up. But you're still here. It's time you started trusting me."

Her gaze returned to his. Her lips firmed but trembled, belying the hard look she was attempting. "Easier said than done."

"Work on it. I owe you. I intend to correct the mistake I made taking you back to Sandoval, but it's not just me involved in this. I may need to call up my teams. I'm not risking my people by walking into something blind. I need to know what you know." He held her gaze. "If I wanted you back with Sandoval, you'd be back with him." Zach stated it bluntly.

She paled at his words. He couldn't regret them if they brought that truth home to her. But he wanted her to trust him. Having her trust was becoming increasingly important to him. She'd been hurt by Sandoval and by Zach himself. He had to take a step back. Give her time to see for herself that she could trust him.

He clasped his hands between his knees and bent over them in an attempt to appear less threatening. "I don't expect your complete trust yet but I have kept you safe and that has to count for something. You can trust me."

Her eyes dimmed. "I've learned that I can't trust anyone."

Her words struck him. The pain behind them. No doubt she'd learned that bitter lesson from Sandoval. She'd given her trust to a man she loved who was supposed to love her and had that trust shattered.

Her emotions were open just now, as hard as Zach believed she was trying to keep them concealed. He could see on her face and in her eyes how badly she wanted—needed—someone to believe in. He wanted her to believe in him.

He bent closer, willing her to see the conviction in his eyes and hear it in his voice. "I'm going to go on keeping you safe. I'll see this through until the threat to you is removed."

The fight seemed to drain out of her. Her shoulders slumped. Zach didn't take the relaxation of her body as an indicator that she believed him and all he'd told her but that she was running on empty. She simply had nothing left in her. She looked lost and vulnerable and it both angered him and made him hurt for her to see her so beaten down.

She closed her eyes tightly and when she opened them her grief was raw. "Rafael is no different from his father." She wrapped her arms protectively around herself.

It was an odd thing to say but it was a start. "Why is he no different, Allison?" Zach asked gently.

"His claims that he wants to change the way his father ruled are all lies."

* * *

Allison's mouth went dry at telling Zach that. Trust him. He had no inkling of the magnitude of what he was asking. How her marriage to Rafael had taught her not to trust anyone.

But as Zach had pointed out, he had taken her away from Rafael. He had brought her to Brock for help. And he had kept her hidden. He was right. While she'd been in the throes of withdrawal for the last three days, he could have opened the doors to Rafael or to the CIA and there wasn't anything she could have done to prevent either from taking her away. Instead, Zach had maintained her secrecy and kept her safe.

He claimed he owed her. The fact he felt a debt eased her a bit, gave her a plausible reason for him offering to help her. If he presented himself as nothing more than a good Samaritan, all kinds of alarm bells would be ringing in her head.

If this were an elaborate ruse he was perpetuating to gain information for Rafael, or now for his CIA contact, she couldn't see it. She no longer believed he planned to hand her over to Rafael or to the CIA. Still, she would not give him her blind trust. She would keep her guard up and not divulge all.

Zach leaned toward her. "How do you know this?"

She chose her words carefully. "I lived in the

country. I saw for myself that Rafael wasn't changing the way things had been done." While that much was true, there was more, so much more that she couldn't risk telling Zach.

A line appeared between his brows. "Reports coming out of that region support Sandoval's claims of wanting to improve his country. We've seen visible positive changes."

Her mouth filled with a sour taste. "Whatever you think you've read, whatever you think you've seen, is wrong."

A nurse entered the room pushing a cart that held a host of medical equipment.

"Time to take some blood, Allison," the nurse said.

Zach ignored the nurse, and his phone which started to beep, continuing to pin Allison with his unwavering stare. Finally, he broke eye contact. Allison could see he wanted to continue their conversation, but he'd gotten all he would from her.

He got to his feet. "I'll be back."

Allison didn't respond. His phone was still beeping. He placed it to his ear and left.

* * *

It was John calling back. Zach walked down the hall, away from Allison's room, and entered a supply room. He closed the door and took John's call. "John."

"Zach, what's happened that you're calling me at this number?" John asked.

"I need all the information you have on Rafael

Sandoval."

There was a pause at the other end of the line. "What's going on?"

"I did a job that went south. I'm going to make it right."

"What kind of job?"

"That's all I can say for now."

John's voice tensed. "You're not making this easy."

"I would if I could. The less you know about this right now, John, the better. You should know that Morse is in this. I can't go to him for what I need. I need to keep Morse out of it."

There was a silence. "I'll expect you to tell me what's going on if it becomes something I need to know."

"You know I will."

"Yeah, I do know that." The tension left John's voice replaced by the trust they shared. "Give me thirty minutes." He ended the call.

* * *

Thirty minutes later, Zach was back on the line with John. "What do you have?"

"I'm sending you a report," John said, "but here are the highlights. Before Rafael's father Enrique died, he had a team of scientists developing a nuclear weapon for him. From what we were able to gather, this weapon was going to be unlike anything we've seen before. When Enrique died, the scientists and the weapon went underground. We don't know where it is. We don't know what stage of development the weapon was at." John paused then added, "We don't know if Rafael Sandoval has taken over for his father and is continuing the project."

"But the CIA thinks he is," Zach said quietly.

"Yeah."

"Zach, there's something else. We had an agent down there undercover trying to find out about the nuke. A few months ago, our guy went off the grid. We haven't heard from him since. We think he's dead."

A burn started in Zach's gut.

"Zach, you there?"

"Yeah. I appreciate the help, John."

"Not completely unselfish. If Sandoval is going ahead with this nuke, I don't need to tell you what he'll do with it. I don't know what you're involvement in all this is, but we're drawing blanks here. I'm hoping you'll find out something we can use."

"Me, too."

Zach ended the call. *Dammit, Allison, where do you fit in all of this?* His gut was telling him she was right in the middle of it.

Zach returned to Allison's room. The door was closed. The nurse was still in with her. John's Intel on Sandoval played over in Zach's mind. He didn't know for sure if Allison was involved in what John had revealed, but better to go with that she was somehow mixed up in this mess and act accordingly. Accordingly to Zach was to move her, get her out of Brock's and into a safe house. He rubbed a hand down his face. He couldn't do that until he got the okay from Brock about her health and then, of course, the okay from Allison herself. For now, though, he could make sure he had a place to take her to.

Zach punched in the numbers for Chase's cell. When Chase answered, Zach said, "Chase, I need you to get a safe house ready."

"Something happen?"

Zach told Chase about his conversation with John.

"Shit, Zach."

"Yeah. Call me when you've got a place set up. I'm going to move Allison as soon as I can."

"I'm on it."

"Chase, there's something else. Morse will be watching Allison's family in case she shows up there. Tell our people. We don't want Morse to spot any of our men near her parents or sister and wonder what our interest is. We don't want Morse to put together that Allison is with me."

"Got it."

Zach ended the call. The nurse exited Allison's room. Now to speak with Allison.

Allison was walking along the edge of the bed, moving at a snail's pace, her face scrunched in concentration and what looked to Zach like discomfort. She was breathing audibly. Beads of perspiration dotted her brow and she raised a hand swiping the moisture away in a gesture of unmistakable impatience. Clearly, she was trying to get some strength back into her limbs but he could see she was in no condition to be exerting herself.

"You shouldn't be out of bed."

The words came out sharper than he'd intended. Allison's head came up. She'd been so focused on what she was doing, he'd startled her. Weak as she was, she lost her footing. Zach closed the distance between them and grasped her shoulders to restore her balance.

"Here. Let me help you," he said.

"I'm fine. I'm okay," she mumbled.

He could see she wasn't. Fatigue had left shadows under her eyes and leeched the color from her face. He wanted to get her off her feet and back into bed but her shoulders slumped in an expression of defeat. Apprehension now replaced the determination that had been in her eyes an instant earlier. She knew she wasn't up to even that small exertion and it scared her. He understood her fear. She was on the run and needed to be at her best to stay alive. She was nowhere near that.

Her shoulders were tense and trembled slightly. Zach gently brushed his thumbs across the taut muscles there.

But there was more than her body to consider. Her spirit was also battered. She needed something right now, even if it was just being able to stand on her own two feet for a moment and have a word with him. Instead of setting her back onto the mattress, he lowered his hands but stayed close in case she staggered.

Allison swallowed. "I know you want to talk about Rafael, but I have nothing more to say."

Zach let that one go for the moment. "I'm not here to ask about Sandoval. I need to speak with you about next steps."

She looked up at him in confusion. "Next steps?"

"We need to get you out of here, Allison. Just as soon as I get the okay from Brock, I'd like to move you."

Alarm filled her eyes and her voice. "Has something happened?"

"No. But we can't stay here too long. The longer we keep you in one place, the greater the risk of Sandoval or the CIA tracking you. We need to get you off the grid. Where no one will find you."

Allison closed her eyes tightly and reached back to the bed. Slowly, she lowered herself onto the mattress. She opened her eyes. Her gaze went to the door then to the window. "You're right. I need to keep moving."

When she attempted to push herself off the mattress to gain her feet, Zach reached out and put his hand over hers. "Easy. I'm not suggesting you leave here this minute. Brock has to clear you first and before you go anywhere, you need to know where you're going. I'm arranging a place for you."

Her spine stiffened and the pulse in her throat began to pound. "Arranging? What makes you think I'd go anywhere willingly with you." Her breathing quickened. "Or does 'willingly' matter to you?"

Zach didn't like that she'd think he would take her anywhere against her will but she'd been through hell with Sandoval. She had every right to be cautious.

With her hand still in his, Zach dropped down so he was crouching in front of her and their gazes were level. "What I should have added when I said I'm arranging a place for you was, 'if you want it'. Contrary to what you think of me, I have never forced a woman to do anything against her will. When I told you earlier that you can trust me, that I will see this through until the threat to you is removed, I meant it. I will do whatever it takes to keep you safe."

Allison stared at him and didn't back down. "And you expect me to believe all of this, everything you've done for me since taking me back from Rafael—bringing me here to Brock's, finding me in the woods, keeping me hidden from Rafael and the CIA—is to repay this debt you feel you owe me? You're going to have me thinking you're an honorable man."

She said it like an accusation, daring him to defy her, but he gave her the truth. "I will do right by you, Allison."

* * *

Zach was right that she couldn't leave Brock's without a clear destination in mind. She could no longer go to where she'd been headed on the night she escaped from Rafael. She didn't have a destination now and didn't know how she'd get to it if she did. She needed a new plan. She needed somewhere to hide and to rebuild her strength. This wasn't over with Rafael. As terrified of him as she was, she needed to see this through with him.

She wouldn't be able to do that in her present condition. Zach was offering her a place to stay. She gnawed her lower lip until she tasted blood.

Could she take what he was offering? Could she believe him in this one thing? Her heart thudded. If she judged him wrongly, it would cost her life and the lives of countless others.

Zach was still holding her hand. His grip was firm but gentle. He didn't appear to be a man capable of being gentle. He was big and formidable. She recalled thinking that of him the first day she'd seen him in the alley. He'd been gentle with her then. Was being gentle with her now. He'd treated her with care since he'd taken her back from Rafael. He could have done all manner of things to her since then. Rather than bringing her here to Brock's, he could have taken her to an isolated location to brutalize her as Rafael had. Who would have stopped Zach? She certainly couldn't have. As weak as she was, she couldn't stop him now if he intended to take her away by force. And if he did, then why consult her at all? Why all this back and forth? He would simply just do it.

Too many questions, she realized. There were too many inconsistencies for her to still believe he would harm her. She'd already decided he wasn't going to return her to Rafael or to hand her over to the CIA.

Zach was still crouched in front of her, giving her time to work out his offer in her mind. She fastened her gaze on his. "Tell me about your plan to leave here."

CHAPTER SEVEN

Four days later, Brock discharged Allison. She was still drastically underweight and weak, but her system was free of the drug and withdrawal was behind her. She needed time to regain her good health but she didn't need to be in a medical facility to do that.

Laurel had given Allison some clothing. Zach placed the small suitcase in the back of his SUV. After Allison thanked Brock and hugged Laurel, Zach led her out to the driveway where his SUV was parked. He'd waited for night to fall before making their departure. The moon was full. It was a clear night.

As he pulled away, he caught the lingering look she gave the clinic. No doubt she was feeling apprehensive about leaving the place where she'd been safe for somewhere that was unknown. "You okay?"

She linked her fingers together in a tight grip and gave him a small nod. Zach believed her grip on her hands was from tension rather than cold, but turned up the heat in the vehicle.

"I need you to listen to me." Zach didn't want to alarm her, but he did want to prepare her. "If I tell you to do something, I want you to do it. No hesitation."

She gave him a sharp look. "You think Rafael could have tracked me here? Or the CIA?"

He cut a glance to her. "No. Like I told you before, if they had, they'd be here but we're about to show ourselves. I'm going to take back roads to our destination, but we'll still be exposed."

"Exposed as in vulnerable." The skin on her hands whitened as she increased her grip. "Rafael will turn over every stone to find me."

Zach hadn't picked up the conversation with her on Sandoval in the last four days. The drive to the safe house was as good a place as any to do that. "Why is Sandoval so eager to find you?"

Allison met his gaze. "I told you. I found out he's lying to the world about his plans for his country."

"How do you know this for sure?"

"Bad timing." She exhaled deeply.

"Go on."

She shook her head. "It doesn't matter. I can't prove it now."

"Why not now? Sounds like you could at one point. What's changed?" When she remained silent, Zach took a different approach. "Where were you headed when you got away from Sandoval?"

She swallowed. "Nowhere in particular. I was just focused on putting as much distance between me and Rafael as possible."

She'd hesitated, so briefly it was barely noticeable, but Zach noticed. Wherever she'd been going, she wasn't ready to share it with him. He could call her on it, but decided to drop it for the moment. They had a long drive. There was time to circle back to it. He pressed on. "What about going to your family?"

"My family is in Washington but regardless, I wouldn't have gone to them. I wouldn't endanger my parents and my sister by going to them. If Rafael knew they were helping me, he'd kill them without hesitation. I can't go to them."

She sounded as if she never expected to see them again. She drew herself in tight as if it hurt too much to talk about her family. There was grief on her face now. It was hard to observe. There was one thing he could assure her of. "Your family is safe."

She faced him. "How do you know?"

"I know where your family is. My people are watching them, protecting them, in case Sandoval makes contact."

She looked at him for a long moment. "Thank you."

Zach nodded. Her shoulders visibly eased and he was glad to relieve her of this worry.

She peered out the front window. "No other vehicles on this road."

Zach had deliberately opted to stay off all interstates. He was driving rural routes that could only generously be called roads. "We're going to stay out of high traffic areas for this trip. I'd prefer we aren't seen and possibly remembered in case anyone shows up out this way asking questions about you."

He'd been over this with her already, but he'd go over it again and again if it reassured her. It seemed to be doing that. She relaxed a little against the seat back.

* * *

A quiet had descended between them for the last several miles as Zach drove them deeper into rural Blake County. Allison took her eyes off the road and focused on him. "How long have you been doing this?"

"About seven years on my own. Five before that for Uncle Sam."

"I'd have thought after being in a war zone, you'd want to get as far away from this kind of work as possible."

Zach smiled. "And do what? Sell flowers?"

Allison shook her head, but her own lips lifted. "Not necessarily, but something non-violent." Even as she said the words she thought, no, Zach was not the type of man who would seek out the kind of job she'd mentioned. There was something savage about him.

"When I resigned my commission with the Navy, I wanted to build a business."

"What exactly do you do?"

"There's no exactly. We're a special operations organization. Military operations. Among other things, we find and retrieve people. We provide protection."

She considered that then asked, "How did you

get started? I don't think this is the kind of thing you print business cards for and pass around."

"I had built a reputation when I worked for the government. Met some people. Most of my business comes from those people."

She could tell he wasn't going to be specific about who "those" people were, but she pressed on, knowing one of those groups. "You mean the CIA?"

"Yeah. We work for our government on jobs that are unofficial. We also take on jobs for civilians or civilian organizations."

"How did Rafael know to come to you?"

"He was referred through a contact of mine."

Feeling chilled thinking of Rafael, Allison hugged herself.

Zach reached out and covered her cold hand with his. "He's not going to find you, Allison. I'm going to make sure of that."

"And this contact? Are you still in touch with him?"

Zach raised an eyebrow. "You can't still be doubting me."

She shook her head quickly. "I wouldn't be here if I thought you were going to hand me over. It's just that I don't like to think I'm being hunted on all sides."

"It doesn't matter how many people are looking for you. They aren't going to find you."

She heard the fierce resolve in his voice and so desperately wanted to believe it.

* * *

Zach was sorry to see the tension return to Allison. Her body had stiffened with it. They'd only been on the road a short while but dark smudges showed under her eyes. She was exhausted, wrung out from her ordeal of the last days, hell, longer than that from what Brock said to cause her body to be so weakened. Though how long, Zach didn't know. Thinking of her condition brought on other dark thoughts, like just how much had she suffered to be so weakened?

When she took her eyes from his and turned her head away from him to look out the passenger window, he hoped she'd sleep.

He tuned the radio to a station that played soothing instrumental music and turned the volume low. As the soft strains of a guitar played on, Allison's head lolled back against the headrest.

Farmland stretched as far as Zach could see. He'd be seeing more of the same for the rest of the drive to the safe house.

Another few miles and they'd leave Blake County and the state behind. Zach glanced over at Allison. She wasn't asleep as he'd hoped. Though her head was still back against the rest, her eyes were open and on the road ahead.

As he took his gaze from her, a large pickup truck drove in front of Zach's SUV, blocking the narrow, dirt road. Zach hit the brakes, shifted to reverse and floored the gas pedal. The SUV shot back, tires screeching.

Allison moved forward as far as the seatbelt allowed. "Zach!"

There were two men inside the truck. The passenger raised an assault rifle. Zach pressed his thumb on the switch for Allison's seatbelt, releasing it, then put his hand on her head and pushed her down to the floorboard. "Stay down, Allison."

Zach expected the man in the truck to aim and fire that mother of a rifle but he didn't. Instead, the truck gave chase. As Zach continued to drive in reverse, two more pickups drove up, cutting Zach off from behind, and blocking his SUV between the trucks. Zach veered to the side to cut across one of the farms but on one side of the road was a deep drainage ditch while on the other a rickety, narrow bridge stretched across a rushing creek. The assholes had planned their ambush well. They'd fenced him in. Zach slammed the brakes.

"Allison, you okay?" he shouted.

"Y-es."

The trucks were left to idle while men climbed down from each. Five men in all. As Zach watched, all five approached the SUV. They all carried automatic weapons held shoulder-high.

Allison's brows pinched together. "Zach, what's going on?"

He could hear the tremor in her voice and her now quick, shallow breaths, but couldn't take his eyes off the men. He reached out and clasped her hand. "The men in the trucks are going to be here in a minute. If it were just me, I'd take them on." He had an arsenal of his own on his person. "But I won't take a chance with your safety." Her hand started to tremble in his. Zach squeezed her a little harder. "Just let me deal with these bastards. We're going to get out of this."

"Rafael's men?"

Zach shook his head. "Sandoval wouldn't have known we'd be here at this moment to overtake us. If these were his people, they'd be behind, following us. This is something else."

Zach tugged her hand and drew Allison up from the floor and back onto her seat. Both his door and Allison's door were yanked open at the same time. Zach released Allison's hand and stepped out slowly, his hands held up in front of him, to find four rifle barrels pointed at his chest. Zach sized the men up. All were big and burly, dressed in jeans and thick, flannel shirts that stretched across massive chests. They bore a resemblance to each other that marked them as family, brothers by the looks of them. What was this?

As Zach looked for the fifth man in their group, he came around to Zach's side of the vehicle, tugging Allison behind him by the hair. His grip on her was white-knuckled. Both of her hands were clamped around the man's fist where he'd wound her hair. Zach gritted his teeth to hold back the need to let loose on the asshole who held her.

The man tapped the barrel of his rifle against Allison's temple. It was a silent warning to cooperate or else. Zach got it. He had every intention of cooperating with these men. So he stood with his hands held up, as two of the men came to stand in front of him. One of them yanked off Zach's jacket, leaving him in a T-shirt, then frisked him, removing his semi-automatics, knives, one grenade and other weaponry from his belt, pockets and ankles.

"That's a lot of fire power you're carrying," the man who'd disarmed Zach said. "We got a tough guy here."

And Zach did nothing when the butt of a rifle was rammed into his gut, then another brought down on his head with enough force to drop him to one knee.

Allison screamed. She jerked against the man who held her. "Please. He's not doing anything. You don't need to do this!"

"Oh, did my brother hurt your boyfriend, sugar?" the man who held her said, confirming his relationship to the other man. He turned to the man who'd hit Zach. "Glen, did you hurt her boyfriend?" He faced Allison again. "Maybe you and me can work something out, sweet stuff, and I'll make him stop."

The man yanked harder on Allison's hair, throwing her head back until her neck was stretched completely. Zach could see her pulse pounding from pain and fear. The asshole gave Allison an up and down look and his eyes darkened with lust. His lips pinched tight with malice. One of the other men whistled.

"Now don't be greedy, Fred," the one named Glen said with a laugh. "We'll all be wanting a piece of that."

Zach clenched his jaw, biting back on a rage that swept through him. It was time he got their attention back on him. Ignoring the pain in his gut and head, he got to his feet. Eyes narrowed, he faced Glen. "I hate to break up the party, but I want to get back on the road."

Glen swaggered to Zach. "Got some place to go, do you?"

Glen struck Zach three blows to the gut, again with the rifle, and this time when Zach went down, he stayed down. Glen rested a knee on Zach's spine, pulled his arms behind him and wound a roll of duct tape around Zach's wrists, binding them, then Glen and Fred jerked Zach to his feet. Allison was shoved into the back of Zach's SUV. An instant later, Zach was thrown in beside her. Two men took the front seats while the others returned to the trucks. A couple of moments later, the vehicles were underway.

* * *

It didn't take long to reach their destination, a dilapidated farm house. Zach and Allison were hauled out of the SUV. Allison noted how the brothers again trained their weapons on Zach as he stood. He was a big man. Despite the fact that he was severely outnumbered and injured, the brothers registered that Zach remained a viable threat.

It was now the middle of the night and flakes of snow began to drift down from the sky. She had Zach's warm jacket, the one she'd taken from Brock's, but the chill air struck her. Zach had to be freezing in just a T-shirt. She shook her head. Cold had to be the least of what he was feeling.

High-pitched squeals shattered the quiet. Pig squeals. Allison looked to the back of the house where the sound was coming from. Too much noise to be coming from just a couple of animals. It sounded like many, many pigs.

Allison was pushed to the door, taking her attention from the animals. Beside her, Zach was shoved hard then Glen brought the rifle butt down on Zach's shoulders again. He stumbled. Allison reached for him to take his weight and lend her support. It was a pitiful effort on her part. She wasn't up to holding his weight. She was barely able to support her own after the last days and the months that preceded them under Rafael's brutal care. Zach must have realized that as well. His body barely brushed hers before he righted himself.

As soon as Zach was steady on his feet, Glen raised the rifle and struck Zach again. The blow landed between his shoulder blades, a solid hit that dropped him to his knees on the hard ground.

Zach looked up at Glen, his look venomous and far from cowed, despite his position on the ground. "What do you want with us?"

"With you?" Glen said. "Nothing. With your woman, here," Glen stroked his chin, "she's more bony and pale than I usually like 'em." He leaned over Allison. "Sweet thing, your man not taking good care of you?" Glen's gaze became avid. "Even so, she's still a prize we hadn't figured on. Isn't that right, boys? Sweet girl, take off that jacket. Me and my brothers want to see what you got for us under there."

The men nodded agreement and laughed. A chill went through Allison. When she didn't immediately comply, one of the men chuckled and started toward her. Allison quickly shed the jacket and dropped it to the ground. She stood, arms around herself, shivering in the sharp wind.

"All this for a piece of ass?" Zach scoffed and slowly regained his feet. "Looking like you all do, I can see why you're hard up."

Be quiet. *Be quiet!* Allison screamed it in her mind, willing Zach to hear her. Why was he antagonizing them? He'd been doing it from the start. Then, she knew why. He'd told her in his vehicle that he'd deal with them and was deliberately drawing the men's attention to himself to keep their attention from her. She felt sick inside that he was suffering to protect her.

"You know, I was going to put a bullet in your head and be done with you." Glen scratched the thick, grizzled stubble on his chin. "But I think I'll hold off. Make you watch us while we fuck your woman."

Allison shut her eyes at the horrible image, but she couldn't let it get to her.

Zach eyed Glen. "Yeah, you could have killed me. Back on the road, you had a direct line of sight. But you didn't. Now why was that?" Zach was silent for an instant, but his hard gaze remained on Glen, then Zach's eyes narrowed. "You didn't want to damage the truck."

"You got a sweet ride, no mistake about that," Glen said. "Vehicles like yours bring in a nice chunk of change. Like I said, your woman's a bonus."

Glen inclined his head to Fred and Fred pushed Zach and Allison into the one-story farm house. Inside, the rooms were narrow and dismal with dull walls and floors and dingy windows. Zach was pushed against a wall. Allison moved beside him.

As Glen reached for her, Zach said, "Why settle for the truck?"

"What?"

"In addition to the truck, I can get you cash—one million."

Glen's eyes fixed on Zach. "What?"

"Yeah, you heard right," Zach said.

"Glen, one—" Fred said.

Glen raised his hand quickly, cutting Fred off in mid sentence. "This is horseshit. You're bluffing." Glen reached for Allison again.

"Am I?" Zach challenged.

Glen paused. "Where's this money?"

Zach raised an eyebrow. "You don't think I carry it around, do you? Even you can't be that stupid."

Glen's mouth went tight at the insult but his greed overcame his pride.

"So where is it?" Glen asked.

"Here in Blake."

"Where?"

"My place."

Glen's face went red with anger. "Nobody keeps one million at their place. Next you'll be telling me it's in your desk at the office."

Zach gave Glen a hard look. "Do I look like the kind of guy who works a nice nine-to-five? You disarmed me. You saw the fire power I carry. What kind of work you think needs that kind of hardware? I'll give you the answer. The kind that deals in cash and pays a lot of it."

Glen rubbed his palm along the barrel of his rifle. "How do I know you aren't bluffing?"

"You don't, but are you willing to take the chance?"

Allison could see that Glen didn't want to take that chance.

"If you touch her," Zach's tone was murderous, "if any of you touch her, you won't see one dime of that money. I'll take it to the grave."

Glen's eyes narrowed. "You aren't in charge here."

Zach held Glen's gaze. "That's right. You are. So decide. Are you going to settle for pocket change with the truck or go for a real score?"

Glen continued to stare at Zach then raised his rifle waist-high. "Move down that hall."

Zach gestured for Allison to precede him so he was now between her and Glen, and Allison led the trio down the narrow corridor. The walls were painted a dull green. The paint peeling. The wood floor was scuffed. Allison came to a door.

Glen gestured to the door with the rifle. "Open it."

When she did, cool air struck her. Wooden stairs descended into a cellar.

"Keep going down," Glen said.

The cellar was cold but not dark. The moon was full tonight and streamed in through large vertical windows. The windows had bars on them, preventing their escape, but the bars did little to filter the bright moon. Even though Glen didn't switch on the light for the lower level, the cellar was lit fairly well and she saw that the room was empty and enclosed by rough cinder block walls and cement floors.

Allison put her hand on the banister and began her descent. Zach's arms were still bound behind him. She glanced back at him anxiously to see if was steady on his feet. Despite his injuries, Zach was sure-footed.

When they reached the bottom, Glen closed the cellar door. As soon as he did, Zach lost his erect posture. He bent over, his teeth gritted in an unmistakable expression of pain.

Allison went to him and wrapped her arms around his waist in case he stumbled. With his arms bound behind him, he wouldn't be able to break his fall. Zach stiffened, again keeping her from bearing too much of his weight. She dug in her heels and braced her shoulder under his arm. "Let me help you."

He released a harsh breath then said, "I'm okay."

He stood against her, taking in deep breaths for a moment, then slowly stepped away and moved to one of the walls.

"How hurt are you?" Allison asked.

"I'm fine."

Obviously that wasn't the truth. He began to move along the wall behind them. "What are you doing? You should be sitting or laying down." Though where would he do that? On the cold cement floor?

"I'm okay."

But he was moving more carefully than she'd ever seen him and when he made a quick move, he gave a little grunt, belying the words. Allison felt useless, helpless to do anything to ease his obvious pain. "Zach, stop that. If you can't lay down, at least stop moving around."

He did come to a stop against one wall, but while he remained in place, he continued to slide his hands against the rough surface. He had to be tearing his skin. As she was about to ask him what he was doing, he brought his hands around to the front of his body. She realized he'd been sawing the duct tape against the sharp cinder blocks.

He yanked off the bits of tape that clung to him and dropped them to the floor. He'd bled on the tape where the cinder blocks had sliced the skin on his wrists.

"All this to get your truck," she stated softly.

He stretched his arms above his head and flexed his fingers. "Yeah. When Glen, Fred and the rest of their brothers drove up, I saw a couple of barns. One of them was open. They had other vehicles in there. We're not the first people they've brought here. There's a pig farm out back. Judging by all that noise, they've got a lot of pigs."

Allison recalled the squeals. "The brothers didn't do anything to disguise themselves from us. They don't care that we saw their faces. I don't need to ask what you think happened to the other people who've been here." She closed her eyes tightly for an instant thinking of the others and what had happened to them.

Zach's hand brushed across her cheek. "We're not going to end up like the others."

She opened her eyes to find his gaze locked on

her. He nodded slowly, never taking his eyes from hers. She felt some shame that he was offering her comfort with all he'd just been through. She wouldn't become a burden to him. He had enough to deal with. "What do we do to get out of here?"

He lowered his hand. "We stall them like I did by dangling the promise of a big score, and we wait. My team will come for us."

She looked up at him. "How will they know where we are?"

"All of the Corrigan vehicles are equipped with GPS tracking devices. Chase will be monitoring mine for our arrival at the safe house. When he sees it isn't parked where it should be, he'll trace us here."

She didn't ask how long before Chase would realize they were in trouble and sound the alarm. She hoped he wasn't too late.

CHAPTER EIGHT

Though she was holding it together, Zach could see that Allison was terrified. Her eyes had gone wide. Her face pale. He took her face between his palms and bent so their gazes were level. "I'm going to get you out of here, Allison. You have my word."

She closed her eyes briefly and when she opened them, reached up and seized his fingers in a tight grip. "With everything else going on, the last thing you need is to coddle me." She shook her head. "You're the one they've hurt. You wouldn't even be in this mess if not for me."

"You aren't to blame." He lifted one corner of his lips. "This isn't the first time I've taken a pounding. It won't be the last and what these assholes have done to me won't kill me. We're both going to walk out of here."

Zach gave her another nod and when she returned it, released her. Every breath hurt. His ribs had taken the worst of it. On the plus side, though, nothing felt broken. He needed to stretch out but there'd be no comfort on the cement floor.

They could have used their jackets. The cellar felt as cold as a meat locker. Allison was visibly shivering. As weak as she was, her body didn't need another assault. He needed to get her warm.

Slowly, he made his way back to the stairs. The wooden steps were by no means warm in the cold cellar but they would be warmer than the cement walls and floors.

He braced one hand on the stair and stretched out his other arm. "You're freezing. Come here, Allison."

She sat beside him. A chill shook her as her bottom connected with the cold step. Zach wrapped his arm around her shoulders and brought her tight against him, ignoring the pain in his side.

She slid away from him a bit. "It can't be comfortable with me pressed up against you. I don't want to cause you more pain."

"It's fine. You won't do me any more damage."

Zach brought her against him once more. She hesitated and he urged her nearer until their bodies were as close as they could get. He brought his other arm up and wrapped that one around her as well in an effort to warm her. She was so small in his arms. She felt delicate and fragile. He tightened his hold.

Allison tilted her head back and looked at him. "How long do you think before they decide to take you up on your offer to get them that money?"

Zach grunted. "They've already decided to go for it. Right now, they're trying to figure out the logistics of it, how to get me and you where we need to be to get the cash."

"You think they'll take me along?"

"It's not going to come to that. My team will come." At her worried expression, Zach added, "But if it did, these assholes have no choice about that." Zach's voice was hard. "You go where I go."

She linked her fingers in a tight grip and said softly, "It would be easier for you all around if you just made a deal for yourself and left me to them."

Zach tipped up her chin farther and looked straight into her eyes. "Not going to happen. You go where I go," he repeated.

He leaned back against the step above. He let out an involuntary groan as his abused ribs and back protested the movement.

Allison shook her head. "If you didn't have me to think about, you wouldn't have taken that beating."

"I don't want you to be worrying about that."

Her gaze on him intensified. "If you were alone, you'd have taken them on, on the road, as you said, and you'd be gone from here."

Zach took in the look in her eyes, the uncertainty, the fear. His heart clenched. Did she think he'd desert her? No wonder if she did, given her experience with Sandoval. If someone she'd trusted—loved—and who must have professed his love for her had hurt her, how could she expect more from a relative stranger? "But I'm not alone," he said. "When I leave here, you'll be coming with me."

She closed her eyes and when she opened them, they shimmered with unshed tears. He couldn't stand to see her laid so low. His gut twisted. He moved his hand up her back and cradled the back of her head. He slid his fingers into her hair, curling them around the soft, silky strands. He held her gaze and eyes open, covered her mouth with his. He'd intended a soft glancing of his lips against hers to reassure her, but as soon as his mouth met hers, he was kissing her in a way that was anything but soft. He felt a surge of possessiveness for her he'd never felt for any other woman. He lowered his hands from her face and wrapped his arms around her. Uncaring about the pain in his ribs, he moved his mouth over hers and crushed her against him.

Allison's mouth trembled against his and Zach yanked back. She'd been through hell with her *husband.* Zach's teeth clenched in anger and disdain at the bastard who had the privilege of being her husband and had shit on that privilege. After all she'd been through with Sandoval, the last thing Zach wanted was to frighten her but, no, he saw no fear in her eyes. Allison was watching him as intently as he watched her. As he stared down into those gorgeous eyes, Zach couldn't resist stroking his thumb once again along her full bottom lip, now made fuller by his kiss. "You go where I go."

She nodded.

"Good."

She didn't move out of his arms, but remained pressed against him. Zach found he liked her just where she was. She looked a little flushed, a little dazed and he found he liked that too.

She cleared her throat. She swallowed and shook her head as if gathering her scattered thoughts, then asked, "In the meantime, while we're waiting for your team, how do we keep the brothers from hurting you more?"

"You let me worry about that. The most important thing right now is to keep them focused on me and not on you."

"At what cost to you. We need a plan."

"I know what I'm doing. We need to keep their focus off you." Allison shivered and Zach could well imagine what she was thinking about these bastards getting their hands on her. "They're not going to touch you," he said fiercely. "They're not going to make a move on you until they either have the money or know they aren't getting it. It's not going to come to that." Zach let her hear the resolve in his voice and let that sink in before he dropped the next thing on her. "I need you to be prepared for something else." He lowered his voice to little more than a whisper. "In addition to keeping them from hurting you, we have to make sure they don't recognize you. You've been photographed by the media standing at Sandoval's side. We don't want these assholes to figure out who you are and decide they can sell you to him."

Allison shivered. He was sorry to have to add to her fear but she needed to know what they were up against.

Zach raised his hand and cupped her cheek. "I've given them something to think about other than you. The thought of that money should keep them occupied until my people arrive."

His shoulders tightened. The operative word there was "should". That's why Zach had dangled such a large sum of cash to the brothers. But if their captors recognized her before Zach's team arrived, Zach worried they would try for an even greater payoff for her from Sandoval than what Zach had offered.

Zach increased his hold on Allison. By now, Chase would have seen that Zach's vehicle was no longer en route to the safe house and would be mobilizing a team. His people would be here by dawn. Zach glanced to the window. There was still too much time before dawn.

* * *

Allison sat against Zach. If one of these men recognized her, Rafael would waste no time getting to them. And if he arrived before Zach's men could get them out ...

She shuddered. Despite what had to be excruciating discomfort, Zach's hold on her tightened. She hated that she was so frightened. Where was the woman she'd been? Rafael may not have broken her, but he'd broken something in her. The thought of returning to him could unravel her if she allowed it. That was the last thing they needed now—for her to dissolve into a quivering puddle of fear.

She had to do better than this—for both of them. It was important to her to hold up her end, to contribute in some way rather than to be a drain on them both. She was so tired of feeling afraid all the time. But despite the pep talk to herself, she couldn't shake the fear that the door would burst open and Rafael would come striding in.

Zach's arm was wound around her, holding her flush against him. He began to rub his hand up and down her arm. "Just a little longer, Allison. We'll be out of here soon."

There was such conviction in the statement and it gave Allison hope to fight back the panic. She needed to be strong now. Despite his stoicism, Zach wasn't sitting as erect as he had been. He was more hurt than he'd let on. She looked up at him. "How are you holding up?"

"I'll live. I need to change position."

He seized the banister with one hand and inserted his other between them, flattening his palm on the step. He grunted as he began a slow, arduous process of getting to his feet. Allison got to her own, arms outstretched to catch him if he stepped wrong and went down, or if not catch him, she'd break his fall when he landed on top of her.

But Zach made it to his feet on his own steam. He took a measured step away from her. His teeth were gritted and despite the frigid temperature in the cellar, sweat beaded on his forehead. Again, she was struck that he'd sustained this beating, without defending himself, to protect her. As long as they were beating him, they wouldn't beat—or do worse—to her. She didn't know what to make of that. She no longer knew what to make of him.

He'd kissed her. Her lips still throbbed from the force of his kiss—throbbed in a good way. That surprised her, no shocked her. When he'd moved toward her and she knew what he was about to do, it shocked her how badly she'd wanted Zach to kiss her. She'd thought Rafael had stripped her of any feelings of desire but he'd only stripped her of desire for him. Despite all he'd done to her, maybe she was still in there … somewhere.

Her stomach rumbled. She hadn't had regular meals from Rafael over the last months and had gotten used to being hungry all the time.

A line appeared on Zach's brow. "Keeping us without food or water will be their plan." The line deepened. "You can hardly afford to skip meals."

She felt her cheeks heat. She knew she looked like the crows had picked her flesh from her bones, but she also knew that Zach wasn't denigrating her appearance. His concern was obvious. "I'll be fine. I've missed many meals and I'm still here."

Zach's frown became a scowl and his jaw went tight. "Was Sandoval's plan to starve you to death?"

"My weight loss went along well with his claim that I was ill. Me looking like this supports what he's been telling the world about me."

"He told me that he'd kept word of your mental illness—" Zach sneered "—under wraps."

"He didn't. The people he wanted to know, he told. Like the senators at the receptions we attended. Rafael told me, warned me, there'd be no help from those people. Mental illness was his excuse if I started saying things about him he didn't want said. I no longer look well which supports his claim that I'm sick. If I died later in South America, only my family would question it and they would be a world away." She closed her eyes tightly at the thought of how close she'd come to dying.

"But you survived. Instead of dying, you flipped him the bird in a solid 'Fuck you'."

Her head shot up and her eyes flew open. Of all the things she'd thought he'd say, she hadn't expected that. Zach, she was learning, was blunt in the extreme and had a way of cutting to the heart of things. He was also right. She had thwarted Rafael. A laugh bubbled out of her and one side of Zach's mouth quirked in a smile.

Zach reached up and stroked his thumb down her cheek. "Now that's a beautiful sound. We need to make sure you have reasons to do that more often."

It was a sweet thing to say and unlike him, she thought. The more time she spent with him, the more she came to see he was not the hearts and flowers type. "I'm not going to let Rafael take me back."

"Sandoval won't take you. Not while I'm still breathing." Zach's tone was fierce.

His declaration, his show of support, of unity, meant more to her than he could possibly know.

Her stomach rumbled again.

"What's your favorite food?" Zach asked.

She didn't need to think about her answer. "Lasagna."

"As soon as we're out of here, I'll make sure you have all the lasagna you can eat."

She played along. "What are you going to have?"

"A steak sounds good. And ice cream."

Allison's lips twitched. "It's winter."

"The season has nothing to do with it. I'll eat ice cream anytime."

Allison smiled. "Okay. What flavor?"

"Doesn't matter. Growing up, Ellen used to surprise me with different flavors all the time. I love them all."

"Ellen?"

"Yeah. Ellen Turner. She's the woman I call 'Mom'."

The love he felt for this woman named Ellen was unmistakable. Allison wanted to ask him about her. About his own mother. Where was she? Allison wanted to know about him and her interest took her by surprise. As did the fact she cared that he'd shared something personal about himself with her.

It was the first time he had. He hadn't told her much, but what he had gave her a glimpse of him beyond the skilled, confident man. He'd trusted her with something of himself. He knew about her. It left her feeling exposed, vulnerable. Knowing something about him, balanced them a little.

A sound at the top of the stairs halted her thoughts and drew her attention. If Zach's intention had been to distract her from their present situation and from her fear for a few minutes, then he'd succeeded. But the reprieve was over.

Allison's heart began to pound and her breath caught. Zach's body tensed. His gaze sharpened and he went on the alert. He reached for her and despite his injuries, pulled her to her feet swiftly, as if she weighed nothing at all, and away from the stairs, placing her behind him. The sound outside the door stopped. Whoever had made it, moved on.

Allison's pent up breath whooshed out, leaving her light-headed. Despite the fact that the cellar was almost as cold as being outside, her hand in Zach's was now slick with perspiration.

Zach remained tensed, his body as still as Allison believed it could be and still be breathing. He appeared to be monitoring the situation. Only after several minutes passed and none of the brothers entered the cellar, did Zach ease his stance.

Fear was still riding her hard. She was still breathing hard. The brothers hadn't come this time, but eventually they would.

Zach released her hand and drew her into his arms. "Easy." His voice was harsh with concern. "Whoever was there is gone. It's okay."

His arms were tight around her. His heart beat steadily beneath her cheek and she closed her eyes, willing herself back from the edge. After a moment, she raised her head. "I'm sorry."

"No need to be."

She moved to step out of his arms, but he held her in place. "You're fine where you are."

The truth was she didn't want to move away from him. With Zach, she didn't feel alone—on her own—and she'd been alone for so long.

Zach rested his chin on the top of her head and said quietly, "This will all be over soon."

He sounded so certain. She raised her head to look at him and asked the question that had been niggling her. "How did the brothers know where to find us? Could someone from your organization be working with them?"

"My people are solid. I don't want you to worry about that. The brothers were laying in wait, looking to ambush someone—anyone—driving the type of vehicle they were after. They weren't waiting for us specifically." His gaze lifted to the window. "We only have to hold them off until my people get here and they'll be here soon. Whatever happens, remember, we're going to get through this."

He never missed an opportunity to reassure her despite the fact that he had to be exhausted and in a great deal of pain. He shifted position slightly and tensed with the movement. Allison went still, riding out the pain with him.

A noise at the top of the stairs had her eyes darting from Zach and to the door.

Zach drew her behind him again, keeping her hand in his. "Stay behind me."

This time the door opened. Light streamed down. Allison peered around Zach's shoulder. The men trod down the stairs, their heavy footfalls as loud as a stampede of cattle.

Glen's doughy face was red and his small brown eyes slitted with anger. Allison's heart rate skyrocketed. Zach's body went rigid and his grip on her hand tightened.

Glen didn't break pace when he reached the bottom of the stairs but kept coming with the speed of a freight train. When he reached Zach, he drove his fist into Zach's middle. Allison screamed. She raised her free hand and grabbed Zach's arm. He staggered but didn't go down. She didn't know how he managed that.

"You been holding out on us," Glen said. "Waving pennies at us, all the while holding onto the crown jewel." He lifted his other fist that was clutching a rumpled newspaper. "All the while you got Rafael Sandoval's wife."

Allison's stomach dropped and fear weakened her knees. Zach must have sensed her terror. He squeezed her hand in a death grip. His message was clear: Keep it together. Don't lose it.

Glen rubbed his chin. "First I thought maybe you stole her from Sandoval so you could ransom her back. That all that fuss you made, putting us off on touching her, was because you didn't want her damaged, but now, I'd say I was wrong about that. You two look tight. Wonder what Sandoval will think of that?" Glen looked at Allison. "A pleasure to meet you, Allison. Nice article on you and your husband. Didn't say though that you were missing. Guess your husband doesn't want that getting out, huh? Newspaper also didn't say where your husband is staying. Now, why don't you tell me where he is and I'll invite him over?"

Allison's breath stuttered.

Glen laughed. "Yeah, I can see you not being anxious to see him again. I'm betting once he finds out what you've done with this man, when he gets through with you, you aren't going to look so pretty." His eyes fixed on Allison and his voice dropped. "You know now I won't hurt you, but if you don't do what I tell you, I have no problem whatsoever hurting him." Glen jerked his thumb at Zach.

Zach's gaze became deadly. "Go fuck yourself."

Glen raised his fist to hit Zach again. Allison shouted, "No! Don't. Please. I'll tell you what you want to know."

Zach's head swung to her. "Like hell you will." His eyes were dark with meaning. He broke eye contact and faced Glen again. Zach's nostrils flared. "The lady has nothing to say to you, asshole."

"Well, that would be a shame for you."

Zach sneered. "You can't kill me. Think Sandoval will thank you for depriving him of the opportunity to pay me back for taking his wife from him? I'll say it again, even you can't be that stupid."

Glen's face reddened and his hands clenched and unclenched with rage. "Yeah, I'll probably get a bonus for handing you over to Sandoval. You're right. I won't kill you. But nothing says I can't mess you up. A lot. Before we're through with you, you'll be begging her to call Sandoval."

As the other two men came forward and seized Zach by the arms, Zach stared at Allison. "Don't tell them anything or everything you've done to get away will have been for nothing."

The two brothers had a tight grip on Zach. They weren't fools and knew if Zach chose to, even injured as he was, he could still put up a fight, but Zach offered no resistance as they led him out of the cellar. Despite Glen's claim that Allison was now off-limits to him and his brothers, she knew Zach wanted them away from her.

As soon as the cellar door slammed shut behind Zach, Glen and his brothers, Allison scrambled up the stairs. She twisted the knob in the hope that in their eagerness to get to Zach or in their anger at his taunts, they may have left the door unlocked. Just what she would be able to do if she could get out of the cellar, she didn't know at the moment. The thought of locating one of the brothers' guns and forcing them to release Zach and herself had her blood pumping. If she'd thought herself incapable of taking a human life, that thought was gone. But, of course, the door was locked.

She didn't think they'd take him out of her hearing. They would want her to be able to hear what was being done to him so she would relent and tell them what they wanted to know. Hearing was enough. She didn't need to see. The mind was a powerful force and could conjure up its own horrors, as well she knew, without her needing to actually see what was being done to Zach.

There was no conversation. The brothers must have realized all had been said that needed to be said. They wasted no time getting to the point of why they'd taken Zach away. The unmistakable sounds of flesh striking flesh became the only sounds.

Tears filled Allison's eyes. She should call out,

tell them to stop. That she'd tell them how to contact Rafael. But she didn't. Zach's words about all she'd done to get away, all he'd done to keep her away, being for nothing, rang in her ears. But was that all of it? Or was it cowardice at being back with Rafael that was getting Zach more hurt? Was this really the best course of action? Tears ran down her cheeks. Despite all her talk of being brave, was she nothing more than a coward, letting Zach suffer unimaginably to prevent her from being returned to the monster she'd married?

Despite blow after blow, Zach made no sound. Allison was now sobbing. It was one thing to agree to stand by and do nothing while another was being hurt, but it was something else altogether to actually do nothing more than bear silent witness. She wasn't selfless and she didn't want to go back to Rafael where she would surely die, but how could she continue to let Zach be hurt because of her? And if she did give in, how much worse would Rafael hurt Zach? The certainty of that halted her breath and had tremors coursing up her spine.

Zach was so silent. Was it his sheer strength of will that kept him from crying out, or had they hurt him so badly he was unable to make any sound? Allison was now trembling, her teeth chattering with that thought.

The door to the cellar was thrown open. Were these animals bringing Zach back? Had they beaten him as much as they dared or risk killing him?

"Allison."

So intent was she on her thoughts of Zach that it took a moment for her to realize that the one speaking was Zach's team member, Chase. *It was Chase.* Zach's people were now here. They were safe. Relief had her stumbling, but she righted herself as Chase reached out to her.

"Allison are you hurt?" he asked.

She clutched his forearms that were covered with combat wear. "It's not me. It's Zach. You have to find Zach. You have to help Zach."

"We have Zach."

"Where is he? How badly did they hurt him?"

Even as she asked the questions, she brushed by Chase intent on finding Zach for herself but Chase stepped in front of her, blocking her exit.

"We're still checking out the surrounding area," Chase said. "Stay behind me. I'll take you to Zach."

A couple of moments later, she saw him. Blood oozed from a cut on his brow and another on his mouth. One eye was swollen and already starting to bruise. He stood between two men dressed similarly in combat gear as Chase. Zach's arms were draped over the shoulders of the two men. Her heart lurched.

Allison went to him. "What did they do to you?" She shook her head at the stupidity of the question but plunged on. "You need to lay down. You need to see a doctor." She heard herself babbling. She looked about her for Glen and the brothers.

Zach gently placed his finger to her lips. "It's over. My men have the brothers. We're safe."

A man, dressed similarly to Chase and the

others, entered the farm house and joined Zach.

"We're secure, Zach," the man said. "We can take you and the lady out of here now."

Zach nodded. He exchanged a look with Chase, who then took Allison gently by the elbow. Another man stepped in front of her and Chase, and Chase began to escort her outside.

She glanced back over her shoulder. "Zach, what about you?"

"I'm right behind you."

Her last glimpse of Zach, before Chase led her out the door, was the two men holding Zach tightening their grip on him in preparation to move forward. He was obviously hurt worse than he'd let on to her.

CHAPTER NINE

Zach watched Allison leave the farm house with Chase. Zach had made sure she wouldn't need to pass Glen and his brothers on her way out. When Zach's men had gone in, the brothers had opened fire. Zach's team had shut them down quickly. The brothers were alive and confined in another part of the house. Allison wouldn't see them again.

Zach needed to get her out of there. He needed to make sure she was kept out of what took place at the farm. He addressed his men, Briggs and Hamilton. "I need a phone."

Briggs reached into a pocket and handed a secure phone to Zach. Zach and Allison weren't the only ones who'd been taken to the farm. Zach's grip on the phone tightened, thinking of the families whose loved ones had fallen victim to the brothers. While Zach's inclination was to feed the brothers to their own pigs, those families deserved to know what had happened to the people they cared about. They were still in Blake County, Mitch's jurisdiction. Zach punched in the numbers to call Mitch.

"Hey," Mitch said a couple of rings later.

"Mitch, I have a situation."

Mitch's light tone instantly became serious. "What's going on?"

Zach told Mitch about the pig farm. "There are vehicles in two barns. Looks like this has been going on for a while."

Mitch blew out a long, slow breath. "How did you find out about this?"

Zach gave Mitch a quick rundown. They were both quiet for a moment taking in the enormity of what the brothers' had done. Zach broke the silence. "I need you to keep these assholes under wraps. I have a woman with me. I can't let that get out. I have to protect her."

"The woman you were telling me about?"

Zach filled Mitch in about Allison. "I can't let her whereabouts get out."

"Yeah, I can see that. I'll take care of it. I'm on my way."

"I'm leaving two of my men here to wait for you. They'll give you any information you need."

"Zach, you okay?"

The worry in Mitch's voice had Zach adding, "I'm good."

"Glad to hear it."

Zach heard Mitch's tone ease in obvious relief. "I'll be away while I see to Allison. I know you're going to want a statement from me. I can't come into the station to do that now. Chase will know how to reach me if you need to talk to me about what went down here."

"I'll let you know after I've seen the farm. We'll touch base at the folks."

"At the folks."

Zach ended the call as Chase rejoined him. "Has there been any word from Morse?"

"Not one. Whatever he's up to, he's not telling us about it."

"No way Morse gave up looking for Allison." Zach's jaw tightened. "What about Sandoval?"

"Nothing new there, either."

"Chase, I need you to go back. Monitor the situation with Sandoval and Morse."

Chase nodded. "On my way. I'll call you with an update."

The sun was up but the day was cold. The ground had a light dusting of snow. Zach took a deep breath of the cool air and swore softly at the discomfort the simple act of breathing caused him.

His SUV was parked where Glen had left it. The three trucks that had brought his team were now parked beside Zach's vehicle. Chase was now getting into one to drive back to the command room. Another would transport some of Zach's men to the safe house now, with the last one left behind for the two men to return to Blake once they'd finished speaking with Mitch.

Hamilton was asking him about his injuries, but Zach didn't respond. His focus was on Allison. Though he knew she was safe, he was tense at having her out of his sight, away from his side. He spotted her in the back of his vehicle. Head down, she sat hunched, her hands clasped in her lap. A blanket was draped around her like a shawl, courtesy of Chase no doubt. She'd been strong but Zach knew this time with the brothers had frightened her. Not only by the threat the brothers posed but she'd been terrified by the prospect that they'd call Sandoval. Zach's hatred of that son of a bitch climbed another notch.

"If we lower the seats in your truck, we can fix it for you to stretch out," Hamilton said. "Me or Briggs can drive while the other one rides shotgun in case there's any more trouble. The lady can ride with the rest of the team in one of the other trucks we drove in here."

Zach's eyes were still on Allison. "No. Allison stays with me."

Zach heard the hard tone in his voice and apparently Hamilton did as well. He dropped the topic.

The pigs had started squealing again. Louder and more raucous. Zach wanted nothing more than to put distance between himself and this place. He turned to Hamilton. "Let's get out of here."

* * *

Allison was relieved when one of the men she'd learned was named Briggs, announced they would be taking a detour to have Zach examined by a doctor they knew. Zach was seated beside her in the back of the SUV. Despite his assertions and his stoicism, she could see he was in pain. Concern for him had her continuously glancing up at him.

The brothers were no longer a threat. She and Zach were two in what appeared to be many people who had fallen prey to Glen and his family. And it appeared she and Zach were the only ones who'd gotten away.

She hugged herself against the goose bumps that now sprang on her arms. Her encounter with the brothers was too fresh and added to that was their threat to call Rafael. The brothers thought they could get money from Rafael but they'd been wrong. What would have happened was Rafael would have arrived with his men, without any money, killed the brothers and just took her. Zach would have been right that Rafael would have executed his form of justice on Zach for taking Allison. But that hadn't happened. It was over. Zach's people had arrived just as he'd said they would.

Zach had one arm around her. Other than when the brothers had been beating him, and the brief time when Chase escorted her to the SUV, Zach hadn't left her side. Briggs was driving and she'd heard Zach give the order for one of the other men accompanying them—Hamilton—to ride on her other side so she sat shielded between Zach and Hamilton. Zach had shielded her. Protected her and paid the price with his body. He'd done everything he could to prevent their captors from hurting her and contacting Rafael.

It was time Zach knew all she did about Rafael. Any doubts she'd had of holding back from him were long gone. Zach would need all the information he could get to keep them safe. To keep them both alive. Zach was now in as much danger as she was. If Rafael knew Zach was helping her, he'd be a target as well.

Now wasn't the time for the conversation she needed to have with Zach. He was hurt. It had waited this long. It would wait until he'd received the medical attention he needed.

Hamilton reached into the back then doled out bottles of water and wrapped food. Allison shook her head at the offerings. Her stomach balked at the thought of putting anything in it even water. She was wound tight from the time with the brothers. Despite the blanket Chase had given her, the heat in the SUV, and Zach's own body against hers, she couldn't get warm.

"You okay?" Zach asked.

Zach had been involved in a discussion about their security with his men but the conversation came to a halt at her refusal of food and his attention was now all on her.

"I'm fine. Just still a little tight," she said. "It'll pass."

"You're not long out of hospital yourself. You need to eat."

"I will. Just not now. The sounds and smells from the pig farm ..." She shook her head. "I can't get them out of my head right now."

Zach's gaze lingered on her. "You sure that's all it is?"

She cleared her throat that was dry from nerves. "I'm fine." When he didn't look convinced she added, "Really. I'll feel better after the doctor's treated you." That much was the truth.

"Zach? Doc Elliot's up ahead," Briggs said.

Zach continued to watch her for another moment, then addressed Briggs. "Pull around back."

* * *

A short while later, Zach emerged from the same door he'd entered. Allison sat forward in the seat as he slipped into the SUV beside her.

"What did the doctor say?" she asked.

"I'm not about to go toes up."

Allison met his gaze but didn't respond. She couldn't get into the spirit of his humor even though she knew he was making light of his injury for her. Beneath the bruising, his face was as pale as the snow now slowly coming down outside the SUV's windows.

Zach brushed hair back from her face. "I'm okay. A busted rib is the worst of it. I'll be fine in a few days." He turned to Briggs. "That snow is sticking. Let's see if we can get to the safe house while it's still daylight."

* * *

The snow had indeed slowed their progress. It was night when they arrived at the safe house, a bungalow made of brick that looked washed out in the faint moon light. The house was set on a sprawling plot of land surrounded by dense trees. The snow further obscured the presence of the house. Anyone not specifically looking for the place would never find it. Which, Allison figured, was the point.

Inside, the first thing that struck Allison were

HIDE

the windows. There were only a handful of them
and they were built high into the walls and small.
The thick trees blocked any light. Allison hugged
herself as her fear of the dark asserted itself, but as
Zach moved around, with her hand in his, he
flipped light switches. Soon, the house was as
bright as a sunny day.

The worn and run down exterior did not
extend to the interior. The walls looked freshly
painted and whoever designed the place gave it
an open concept with a wide space divided into a
kitchen and a living area. Zach passed the kitchen
and led them directly into the living room.

A couple of couches and thick arm chairs in
deep earth tones that looked large enough to
accommodate Zach and the other large men of
his team, should they decide to sleep there, were
in the center of the room. A huge flat screen TV
was mounted on one wall and a stone fireplace
had been built into another.

Zach's men strode in behind Allison. They
dropped their gear and their weapons on any
available surface. Zach released her and did a slow
walk through. Eyes narrowed, he surveyed their
surroundings.

When Zach had been all over the place, he
stopped at what looked like an instrument panel
where he began pushing buttons for what Allison
guessed was some kind of high-tech security
system. Once he was satisfied, he spoke into a
mic on his shoulder.

"Lauder. Vox. Check in," Zach said.

"All quiet," one man said.

The second man, Allison didn't know which

was Lauder or Vox, gave the same response. Zach exchanged another word with the two men then ended that conversation and spoke to the men in the room.

"Hamilton. Nash. You're up next to relieve Lauder and Vox on the perimeter," Zach said. "Keep to your usual shifts."

The men nodded agreement. Zach turned away from them, leaving them to speak between themselves, and came to where Allison stood by one wall.

Gently, he cupped her shoulders. "Bedrooms are down that hall. There are four of them, each with its own bathroom. You can take your pick."

She looked up at him. "What about you? You've been awake longer than I have."

"I've got some things I need to do then I'll sleep. Let's get you to bed."

She took the first room she came to, this one decorated in shades of blue with a huge bed. She was noticing a pattern here. The furniture was all large. Clearly, the men didn't like to be cramped. In here as well, the windows were small and built high on the wall letting in little light. But Zach had reached in ahead of her and turned on what turned out to be another bright light.

Clearly, he'd noticed her need for the lights. The weakness shamed her but to save her pride she couldn't turn them off.

"I'll get the bag Laurel gave you and leave it in here," Zach said. "Catch some sleep. By the time you wake up, food will be ready. You should find whatever girly things you need in the bathroom."

"Girly things?"

Zach shrugged and stuck his hands in his pockets. "I asked Chase to stock up on that stuff."

The lights. The girly stuff. The care he was taking of her. It was all so much. She clutched his shirt and buried her face in his chest. "Thank you." The word came out breathy. She felt choked by emotion.

He wrapped his arms around her and brought her against him so tightly she had to be hurting him. He didn't ask her to elaborate. Maybe he knew just what his concern and his thoughtfulness meant to her after not having either.

He reached up and touched her face. His hands were large and rough but his touch was infinitely gentle as he brushed the pad of his thumb across her cheek. He looked down at her with tenderness that made Allison's heart ache, then lowered his mouth to hers.

Gently, he kissed each corner of her mouth before settling on the center. His tongue swept across her lips slowly as if requesting entrance. Allison gave it and he caressed her tongue lightly with his.

She closed her eyes and dug her fingers into his hard biceps. She swayed against him, as caught up in him as he appeared to be in her.

He kissed her long and thoroughly then framed her face between his palms and just looked down at her. After a time he said, "I'll be back with your clothes."

Zach closed the door behind him and Allison went into the bathroom. The tub was also immense and looked inviting. A long soak might ease her nerves. She filled the tub then eased into it. The warm water, soap and shampoo felt wonderful, but by the end of it, she felt exhausted, as if she'd done far more than she had.

She washed her underthings in the bathroom and left them to dry. The thought of having to put on the clothing she'd worn for the last two days was less than appealing, then she spotted the small suitcase with the things Laurel had given her. Zach had left it just inside the door.

She took fresh underthings, a pair of jeans and a cotton shirt from the suitcase. Laurel was taller than Allison and Allison wound the pant legs back so she wouldn't trip on them. Laurel was willowy but in Allison's current body weight, the clothing sagged on her. Allison looked away from her near-skeletal figure.

Despite the bath, she wasn't going to be able to sleep. Nerves had her stomach in knots and her head pounding. She whirled at a knock on the door. Zach entered the room.

"Food's ready," he said. "Do you feel up to eating now or do you want to wait until after you've slept?"

"I'll go with you."

Zach took her hand in his and led her to the kitchen. The room was painted a lemon yellow and the many light fixtures made it daylight bright. All manner of appliances made it a cook's delight.

The clock on one wall showed the time to be after midnight. The men who weren't on watch were gathered there. Zach introduced them as

Nash, Braddock, McMurtry and Connolly. They were seated with Hamilton at a large wooden table while Briggs grilled thick steaks.

Hamilton turned to her. Both his face and his head were perfectly shaved. "Allison, right on time. Briggs isn't much of a soldier." Hamilton grinned. "But he's one damn fine cook."

Briggs raised his eye brows. His eyes glittered with amusement as he looked up from the meat and volleyed back, "Saved your ass a time or two, Ham."

Hamilton laughed. "In your dreams. Zach only keeps you around because you can cook."

Hamilton looked back at Allison, who had yet to take a seat. He rose from his own and pulled out a chair for her. "Come, sit down."

Allison's stomach clutched at the smell of the food. She laced her fingers in a tight grip, determined to get through the meal. "What can I do to help?" she asked.

"It's all ready," Briggs said and carried a steaming platter heaped high with meat, potatoes and vegetables to the table. "Zach said you like lasagna. I'll have that for you tomorrow."

Before she could reply not to go to all that trouble, Hamilton spoke up again.

"You heated bread too." Hamilton gave an appreciative sigh and snagged a roll as Briggs set a basket beside the platter.

"As my Italian grandmother used to say, 'Buon Appetito'," Briggs said.

Allison's eyes widened on the meat on the platter, cooked to varying degrees, some rare and still swimming in its own juices. Her stomach heaved. She pressed a hand to her mouth and bolted from the kitchen.

CHAPTER TEN

Allison made it to the washroom that adjoined the bedroom she was using. She bent over the toilet, her body shaking with spasms. She hadn't eaten anything but bile came up in painful heaves.

Zach came in after her. "Allison?"

"Go away." She called back to him.

Ignoring her, he crouched behind her. He held her hair back from her face and wrapped an arm around her middle, taking her weight. After a time, even the bile stopped coming up. The bout of sickness left Allison feeling limp and shaky. Zach eased her back against him then down onto his lap on the floor of the bathroom and gently brought her head beneath his jaw.

She lay against him, too tired to move, then she recalled his injured ribs. She drew back but Zach continued to hold her. "Let me get off you, Zach. I must be hurting you."

"You're not hurting me."

She didn't believe him and slowly extricated herself from his hold. On shaky legs, she made her way to the sink and fished mouthwash, a tooth brush and paste from the cupboard beneath the sink. Zach came up behind her. He rubbed her shoulders while she cleaned her mouth, then handed her a towel from the same location when she was done. She made her way back to the bedroom and laid down on the bed, feeling wrung out.

Zach sat beside her on the mattress and stroked damp hair off her brow. "Better?"

She nodded.

"Feel like some ice water?"

Nothing sounded better at this moment. Again she nodded. He left her briefly and went into the kitchen, returning with a glass. He held it for her and braced an arm at her back while she drank. Allison was surprised by how good it tasted and that she drained the glass.

"More?" he asked.

"No, that was enough."

"You're wound up. No wonder." His mouth went flat. "You're in a strange house. Again. After a frightening experience with the brothers. I'd be surprised if you weren't tense."

Despite the anger she could feel coming off him, he continued to stroke her gently. Other than to leave her to get the water, he hadn't stopped touching her since she'd been sick. Maybe he realized how badly she needed the contact to assure her that she was safe.

She wanted to believe she was safe. She wanted to be free of the tension and fear she'd known for far too long. "I'm being silly. I know I'm safe here. I just ... " She let the sentence trail off and shook her head.

"Not silly at all. You haven't had any reason to feel safe for a long time. I want you to know though, you are safe here. I'll be sleeping in here with you. Yes, the house is secure and my men will make sure it stays that way, but I want you to know you can sleep without worrying. You won't be alone in here. I'll be right here on the floor by your bed and I sleep light."

He was going to all lengths to make her feel safe. "Thank you," she whispered.

He raised his hand from where it had been on her shoulder and gently passed his thumb along her cheek. "You're welcome."

He was so strong and capable, it made it easy to forget he was hurt. "You need to be taking care of yourself not babysitting me." She realized he hadn't even had a chance to attend to his own comfort with some sleep or even a shower and a change of clothing. He still wore the jeans and T-shirt he'd had on since they left Brock's. "You should be stretched out."

"How about we both stretch out? There's got to be something on the tube."

She didn't want to try to sleep where they would both be silent and she'd be alone with her thoughts. She felt pathetically grateful for the invitation and nodded.

Zach took her hand and led them both to the couch. The living room was in darkness. Her breathing hitched but he immediately switched on the overhead light. She couldn't even enter a dark room without her insides cringing. She was a disaster.

There wasn't anyone in this room or in the kitchen. The men may have finished eating and gone to bed or more likely, they'd made themselves scarce. She hoped she hadn't chased them from their meal.

She felt a pang of guilt that Zach hadn't eaten and that she was keeping him awake. He had to be asleep on his feet.

Zach flicked on the remote. An old black and white movie came on. He didn't change the channel but left it there on low volume and tossed the remote onto the armchair beside them. He plumped a couple of pillows and settled back with an audible groan.

Wary of jostling him Allison tried to remain still seated beside him, but she shifted uncomfortably against the cushion. She couldn't seem to find a good spot. Not the fault of the couch. She was restless, on edge.

"How about some warm milk?" Zach's voice pulled her from her thoughts. "I don't know if that's the thing to have after you were sick, but if you feel up to it, I think we can find some milk around here."

She didn't know if she'd be able to keep milk down either, but it seemed so normal to be speaking of things like warm milk. Nothing had been normal in her life for a long time. She wanted to try to stomach the drink. "I'll make it. You stay put."

She found the milk, a small pot and two mugs and got the milk heating. Despite the heat coming off the stove, she felt chilled to the bone. She couldn't help but fear this night was some sort of a reprieve, that in the morning she'd be back with Rafael.

"Allison?"

She sucked in her breath at the sound of Zach's voice and hated that she could so easily be back in that dark place with Rafael. By the way Zach was looking at her, she believed he realized she'd zoned out as well. What had Rafael told Zach to gain his help in finding her? That she was mentally ill. Maybe that diagnosis was no longer off the mark.

"The milk is almost ready." Her voice quavered. Zach was half off the couch and on his way to her. She cleared her throat, tried again. "No, don't get up. I'll bring it over."

* * *

She sounded as if she were choking. A small tremor went through her and her eyes filled with tears. She lifted both hands and covered her face.

Seeing Allison in such distress struck Zach to his core. He left the couch and went to her. He turned off the stove she'd left on, then took her in his arms.

"I'll just go back to the bedroom. I'll go now." Her voice, thin, hoarse, defeated, broke.

She pushed weakly against his chest in an effort to break his hold but he wouldn't release her and let her suffer this alone. "You're not going anywhere."

"I'm so tired of being afraid of Rafael," she said

in a voice that trembled.

She burrowed into Zach, gripping the front of his T-shirt and pressing her face against his chest. Bone-jarring sobs tore through her. He pressed her closer. He wasn't a man who comforted women or certainly not often. There were a few exceptions, like Ellen who was his mother in every sense of the word. He would go to the mat for the women he considered his sisters-in-law, Mitch's wife, Shelby, Ben's wife, Caroline, Gage's fiancée, Mallory and John's wife, Eve. And though she could hardly be called a woman yet, he could never stand by while three-year-old Sara, Mitch's daughter, was in the slightest discomfort. But this, this with Allison, was something else altogether for him. Her situation made him angry and made him hurt for her.

He went on holding her while she cried. Eventually, she had nothing left in her and stopped. She drew back from him but kept her head down.

He nudged her chin up with the back of his finger so he could look at her. She was as white as the milk on the stove. "Allison?"

She drew back a bit from him. She reached for a tissue from the box on the counter and wiped her face, then balled the tissue, holding it to her eyes in a loose fist.

The mere thought of Sandoval was enough to bring her to this. Zach's anger went white-hot that she was so hurt. Anger and protectiveness. She was a job that had gone wrong and yeah, he felt responsibility over that, but he'd be fooling himself if he told himself that was all this was.

Somehow it had become more. What more or how much more, he didn't know. He couldn't define it and he couldn't explain it. All he knew was that anyone who would hurt her again would have to go through him. Hadn't he just stood between her and the brothers?

Gently, he lowered her hand from her eyes. He stroked the hair back from her face and tilted her chin up. Her eyes were red and puffy. Her face ravaged and tear stained. It pissed him off all over again and had his heart clenching. "Allison?" he repeated.

She hunched her shoulders, drawing in on herself. "I'm okay now. I didn't mean to let go like that all over you."

She tried to turn her head in unmistakable embarrassment, but he held firm. "We're past the point where you would feel embarrassed with me."

She met his gaze then nodded slowly. "You're right. You've seen me at my worst."

Zach looked directly into her eyes. "I've seen you go through the worst and come through it all."

Her lips trembled but to Zach's relief, curved in a small smile.

"Do you always know the right thing to say?" she asked.

He laughed. "I've never been told that before. Words really aren't my thing." He wrapped his arms around her and when he brought her against him, she pressed her head underneath his jaw and put her arms around his waist, gripping him. Her fierce hold on him made him want to move mountains for her. "You're a strong woman, Allison. If you weren't we wouldn't be here. You need to give yourself more credit." He pressed his lips to her brow in a long kiss.

Against his chest, she said softly, "Who are you, Zach Corrigan?"

She sounded amazed and it knocked him off-balance a little. He brought one hand to her face and gently held her cheek. The hope in her eyes dug a little hole in his heart. "I'm the man who's going to make Rafael Sandoval pay for ever hurting you, and then I'm going to make sure he never hurts you again."

He brought his lips to hers in a kiss as fierce as his vow. Allison made a little sound in her throat then curled her fingers around his wrists, holding him in place, and kissing him as fiercely.

He wanted to go on kissing her, but she was asleep on her feet. He lifted his mouth from hers, but couldn't resist touching her one more time.

He brushed his thumb across the place he'd been kissing. "Our milk is getting cold. How about we take it to the sofa?"

Allison nodded.

They settled on the couch and drank in silence. Allison's eyelids were drooping by the time she took the last swallow, but she made no move to return to her bed. Zach remained where he was as well. So they'd spend the night on the couch. Fine with him.

He took the almost empty mug from her before she dropped it and set it on the end table alongside his own mug. He raised his arm and she cuddled against him, resting her head against his chest. He suppressed a groan as her body made painful contact with his but he wouldn't move her. He lowered his arm and wound it around her, anchoring her to him. After a time, her body went slack against his. She was asleep. It was enough for Zach that he'd been able to give her that, some peace so she could finally shut down and sleep. Right at this moment, he couldn't think of anything that was more important to him than that.

* * *

Allison woke alone on the couch. She was wrapped in a thick blanket and lay on her side on the deep tufted cushions. Zach must have awakened earlier and tucked her in before leaving her. She felt a tug of embarrassment at the way she'd cried all over him last night, but he was right. He'd seen her at her absolute worst when in withdrawal. They were long past the point of feeling embarrassment.

She heard soft sounds coming from the kitchen. She couldn't see that area over the armrest of the couch. Whoever was in there must be trying to keep the noise down. As she thought that, Zach came around the couch holding two mugs of what smelled unmistakably like coffee.

"Morning." He smiled. "Thought you might be ready to wake up."

He set the mugs down on the sturdy coffee table then sat on it, facing her. She pushed her hair, that was wild after the night, back from her face and sat up. Zach looked fresh from a shower.

She could smell soap and shampoo. His hair was damp and combed back from his face. He hadn't bothered to shave. Hadn't shaved since before their encounter with the brothers and now had a few days of stubble on his cheeks and jaw. He looked rugged and untamed. That word fit him like skin.

Other words popped into her mind. Handsome. Sexy. She was having a healthy reaction to him. She was not physically afraid of Zach and if ever there was a man who was physically intimidating, Zach was it. He was big, towering over her, and solid. She'd been in his arms and had felt how hard and muscular he was. Rather than feeling intimidated by his sheer size and strength, she felt attracted. Something she'd questioned ever feeling for a man again.

"One of those for me?" She pointed to the mugs of coffee on the table.

Zach handed her a mug then picked up his own. "I hope you're hungry. Breakfast is almost ready."

"I'm starving."

A look came into Zach's eyes that was part anger and part sadness. "There'll be no more of that."

Her heart gave a tug over his continued concern for her well-being. Softly she said, "I'll go freshen up then I'll help with breakfast."

By the time Allison returned, breakfast was ready. The men who were absent from dinner last night were now seated at the table. Vox and Lauder. Both had long hair. Lauder's was loose on his shoulders while Vox tied his back with a thin leather string. Tattoos decorated one of Lauder's arms from shoulder to wrist. Allison exchanged greetings with the men then took a seat beside Zach.

Briggs took some more good natured ribbing on his culinary skills from Vox and Lauder that Allison had to agree were exemplary. The man was a master chef and that morning, in addition to bacon, ham and eggs, he'd prepared fresh fruit pancakes the likes of which Allison had never tasted before. If the men ate like this on all their missions, it was a wonder they didn't outweigh the house.

There was a period of silence as they all dug in. Vox finally broke the quiet.

"Ham is sure missing out, freezing his ass on watch." Vox laughed. "It's as cold out there as a witch's—"

Lauder cleared his throat and tilted his head in Allison's direction.

Vox glanced at Allison and coughed behind his hand. "That's to say, it's cold out there." A gleam lit his eyes. "Think I'll go and let him know what he missed." Vox pushed his plate back then rubbed his hands together and let out a maniacal laugh before leaving the table. Laughing as well now, Lauder and Briggs followed Vox out of the kitchen.

Allison forked up a bit of pancake. She was stuffed but couldn't resist one last bite. "I like your men."

Zach nodded. "They're good."

"Are they all former military, like you?"

"Yeah, we were all SEALs."

She set her fork down and propped her chin on the back of her hand. "What about your family? Were they military as well?"

Zach went silent for a minute. "No. My mother called herself a hostess but she was a prostitute. I don't know who my father was. I don't think she did either though there were a lot of men over the years she wanted me to call 'Dad'. My mother never met a man she didn't like."

Allison's eyes grew soft in sympathy. "That must have been hard."

His mouth went flat for an instant then he said, "It wasn't a picnic, but I survived."

Allison believed there was much he was leaving out of those years and her admiration for him grew at his way of thinking. Life happened, both the good and the bad. You dealt with it and moved on. She wanted to be able to do the same when it came to Rafael once this was over. Move on and never look back.

She didn't want to pry, but she wanted to know about Zach. All about him. "When we were in the brothers' cellar, you mentioned a woman named Ellen?"

Zach didn't appear to mind her question or appear reluctant to talk. He smiled and again Allison saw the love he felt for this woman.

"Yeah. Ellen Turner," Zach said. "She's the mother, technically stepmother, of my oldest friend, Mitch. Mitch and I met in second grade. I started a fight with him in the school yard. Mitch bloodied my nose." Zach laughed. There was no rancor in the statement. "We became friends after that.

"My mother took off that same year and Mitch's folks, Ed and Ellen, took me in and raised me as their own. They didn't make any fanfare about it. Just moved me in. Put a bed for me in the room their two boys, Mitch and Ben, shared. I didn't always make it easy for them, but from the minute I walked through their front door, I was one of theirs and they never let me forget it. Never gave up on me." Zach shook his head as if at the wonder of that. Grinning, he rubbed the stubble on his chin. "They gave me the same praise when I did well and," Zach laughed again, "the same grief as their sons when I took a wrong turn."

"They sound wonderful," Allison said softly.

"The best."

Talk of family made Allison long for her own. Thanksgiving was in a little more than two weeks. She'd never missed that holiday with her parents and sister. This year, they'd be celebrating without her and no doubt wondering why she and Rafael had not made the trip to spend the holiday with them as he'd promised. Another promise he'd never intended to keep. As far as broken promises went, this one was minor. He'd broken so much worse.

Her parents would at least expect her to call. She knew she couldn't call them. For their own safety, she couldn't make contact. But not hearing from her would hurt them.

They had no way of knowing her marriage was a nightmare. That she'd married a monster. Better they didn't know. As long as they remained unaware of what her life had become, they would be safe. As long as she stayed away from them, Rafael would have no reason to hurt them.

Laughter and conversation came from the doorway. Briggs, Lauder and Vox were stomping their boots free of the snow clinging to them. Not long after they were back in the kitchen, filling mugs with coffee.

Allison left the table and began clearing dishes and pans. The men joined in and the clean up was soon done.

Vox rubbed his hands together. "Who's up for gaming?"

"Hell, yeah," Lauder said.

Briggs nodded agreement. "I'm in. Zach?"

Zach topped up his mug with coffee. "Sure. Allison, you up for a game?"

"I've never played video games before."

"We'll show you," Briggs said.

"I'm sure you don't want to spend your time teaching me. I'll slow you all down."

"You can't be any worse than Lauder was when he started," Vox said.

Lauder flipped him off. "That's because I never spent my down time holed up in my apartment with make-believe people. I went out and met the real deal."

"Yeah. Yeah," Vox said. "Bottom line. You sucked. Now we gonna play or what?"

* * *

Briggs took Allison by the hand and led her to

the couch. Allison glanced over her shoulder at Zach who trailed behind her, but Zach noted she was smiling. Not long after, the game was underway. Zach found himself watching Allison. She sat on the end of the couch, face drawn in concentration. She proved to be adept and was clearly enjoying herself. Every time her laugh rang out, Zach felt a smile on his face as well.

They broke for lunch then Lauder and Vox went to catch some sleep before they took the night patrol. Briggs promised Allison lasagna for dinner then went to do his own thing.

Allison glanced up at the window. "I think I can see a few snowflakes on the glass."

Her tone was wistful. How long had it been since she'd spent any time outside? Yeah, she'd been out while traveling, first with him when they'd been waylaid by the brothers, then after on the way here. But being on the run wasn't being outdoors. Zach felt fury for all she'd been subjected to.

He led her to the hall closet where he retrieved warm jackets, gloves, and boots. Allison had only his jacket and the athletic shoes Laurel had given her and Zach had made sure Chase included a new jacket for Allison, a hat, gloves, and boots in her size when he was getting the girly things. Her boots were lined up among several sets of mens' boots.

"We're going somewhere?" Allison asked as he held her jacket for her.

"Yeah." His voice was tight. The anger he felt for her mistreatment was still close to the surface. "We aren't going far. Just into the yard and we'll stay behind the cover of the trees."

When she was dressed in the outerwear, he took her hat from a top shelf and put that on her, carefully tucking her hair beneath the thick wool. He put on warm clothing as well then led her to the room he'd designated to store the teams' arsenal.

All manner of weapons were in this room. They were safe in the yard. He wouldn't risk Allison if they weren't, but nowhere was one-hundred percent safe and Zach took no chances. He selected a couple of handguns and holsters then secured the weapons at his shoulder and ankle. He added a vicious blade then took Allison to the rear door of the house.

"Hamilton. Nash. Check in," Zach said into the mic he affixed to his jacket.

"Here, boss," Hamilton said.

"Something up, Zach?" Nash asked.

"What's the status out there?"

"Clear," Nash said.

"Clear," Hamilton echoed.

"I'm coming out with Allison. We'll keep to the back porch. If anything moves beyond that perimeter, shoot it."

"Affirmative," both men said in unison.

Zach preceded Allison out the door. He did a sweep of the immediate area, though he didn't expect to find anything. His men were the best at what they did. All was clear and he held the door for Allison to join him outside.

The yard was enclosed on all sides by Evergreens that were now powdered with snow that glistened in the sun. Snow covered the yard and back porch. More was falling, removing all trace of the footprints left by Zach's men.

Allison took a deep breath and turned her face up to the sky. Zach came up behind her and stood with her back to his chest. He put his arms around her to keep her warm. Allison didn't speak. She appeared lost in her own thoughts. After a time, she turned in his arms. Her eyes gleamed with mischief and she broke away from him.

Walking backward she gave him a smile that was now as full of mischief as her eyes. "Know what I love most about snow?"

Zach smiled. "What do you love most about snow?"

"Snowballs!"

In a flash she reached down, grabbed a handful of snow and formed a small ball. She tossed it at him. The ball broke against his shoulder.

Zach grinned. "Baby, you don't know what you just got yourself into. I'm the snowball king."

Allison danced back on her toes, no mean feat given the depth of the snow. Laughing she held out her hands, fingers wiggling in challenge. "Bring it."

Zach lunged for her. His ribs protested the sudden and sharp movement but he didn't care and didn't back down or slow down. Allison let out a small shriek and then the snowball fight was on.

As she dodged Zach's pitches and threw her own, Allison's squeals of laughter were something Zach was sure he'd never forget. He'd do a lot, he realized, to cause her to laugh like that.

Not long into their play, Allison's breathing became labored. Her body was still recovering. Zach wiped snow from his face then put a halt to the game by pulling her close and rubbing his hands softly up and down her arms. "Let's get you inside."

CHAPTER ELEVEN

Zach was glad to see Allison eat a sizeable portion of Briggs's lasagna for dinner. Zach intended to make sure she ate well and would ask Briggs to prepare that meal again while they were here.

After, while Briggs was regaling Allison with his grandmother's secret recipe for her favorite food, Zach went into the living room and called Chase.

"Any word on Sandoval or Morse?" Zach asked.

"No. Whatever they're doing, they're doing it quietly."

Zach rubbed the back of his neck. "I don't like that we're in the dark. They've forced us to go into hiding. We're not doing anything to resolve this situation. I don't like playing cat to their mouse. We need a few days to hole up, let Allison get some of her strength back, then we need to make a move, Chase."

"You got something in mind?"

Zach looked to the kitchen where Allison was smiling at something Briggs said. Zach had to make sure at the end of all this Allison was safe. "I'm working on it. This has gotten complicated."

"You okay?"

"Fine."

"Something on your mind?"

Zach released a sigh. "You mean other than protecting Allison from Sandoval and the CIA?"

"Yeah, other than that."

Zach could now hear laughter in Chase's voice. "Glad I'm amusing you. Like I said, this just keeps getting more complicated."

There was a sound of foil tearing, then Chase crunching what sounded like potato chips and chuckling. "You still talking about the mission here? Or are we on to something else?"

"What, are we going to sit around like a bunch of high school girls talking about our feelings? Of course I'm talking about the mission." But he wasn't sure that was all he was talking about.

"Seriously, Zach, you can walk away from this one. You're hurt. You can use the downtime. Briggs, Ham and the rest are more than capable of protecting Allison and I could come there. You can sit the rest of this one out."

No way in hell was he going to do that. His humor gone, he said, "Allison stays with me." Zach all but snarled it. "Got that?"

"Absolutely. It's your call."

Chase wasn't trying to piss him off. Zach recognized he was touchy when it came to Allison and eased his tone. "Anything else?"

"One thing more. Mitch called. He said they

found a shit load of evidence at the farm. The brothers rolled on each other and pled out. There's not going to be a need for you or for Allison to testify against them."

"I'm glad of it. Keep me posted on Morse and Sandoval."

Zach disconnected and clipped his phone to his belt as Allison came out of the kitchen carrying a bowl piled high with ice cream. When she reached him, she held it out. Smiling she said, "You didn't have any dessert."

A slow smile curved Zach's lips. "I never turn down ice cream." He scooped up a spoonful of the chocolate chunk and offered it to her. Instead of eating it, her eyes filled with tears. Alarmed, Zach plopped the bowl and the spoon onto an end table. "Hey?" He put his arms around her.

Allison wound her arms around him, holding him with what felt like all the strength she was capable of.

"I didn't think a man like you existed," she said.

The way she said that made him ache for her and for all the hopes and dreams that she'd had crushed, no doubt by Sandoval. A job? Yeah, Allison had started out that way, but she was more than that to him now. He had feelings for her, feelings that were growing deeper. Seeing her anguish felt like a knife to his gut.

He pulled away slightly. Gently, he lifted his hands and framed her face. "Where's this coming from, sweetheart?" Certainly not from offering her his ice cream. No, this was something else.

"I'm terrified of you, Zach."

He felt as if his blood had run cold. Brows drawn together he looked into her eyes. "Baby, I would never hurt you. I won't ever hurt you."

"No." She shook her head quickly and her fair hair swept over her shoulders and back with the strength of her denial. "That's not what I mean. I know you won't hurt me physically. It isn't that."

Relief staggered him. He stroked her cheeks with his thumbs. "Then what?"

She looked at him, her eyes wide and vulnerable and the knife in his gut twisted, cutting deeper.

"I'm terrified of how I feel when I'm with you," she said. "Of how you make me feel."

Zach's hold on her face tightened just a little. "This is no longer about me seeing you safe because I made a mistake when I returned you to Sandoval. This is about you." There was the truth of it. "I care about you and all that matters to me—everything that matters to me—is making sure Sandoval never gets near you again."

Tears spilled onto her cheeks.

"Baby, no. Don't cry." Zach pressed his lips to the damp spots on her face.

"I'm not the woman I was, Zach. I may never be again. Rafael broke something in me, something I may never be able to fix."

It took all Zach had to rein in the rage that built with every tear she shed. But this wasn't about what he was feeling. This was about her. He wanted to tell her she was going to be all right. That what that son of a bitch had broken would heal, but words were empty. He had nothing to back them up. Sandoval had put her through hell. Zach was sure he still didn't know all of what that bastard had done to her.

"And I gave him the power to hurt me."

She spoke so softly, Zach wasn't sure he'd heard her right. "What?"

Her beautiful eyes shimmered with tears. "I chose Rafael. I chose to marry him."

Over her head Zach saw Briggs and Nash step into the living room. They must have seen or heard Allison's distress. Their brows were lowered. Their faces pinched tight with worry. Zach shook his head slowly and the men left.

Zach looked into Allison's eyes. "And you believe you're somehow responsible for what happened to you? For what he did to you?" She was blaming herself. Zach was no shrink but it was obvious Sandoval's abuse had gone deeper than the physical. Zach couldn't stand that she was in such pain. He pulled her close again, holding her as tightly as he could without hurting her. He closed his eyes briefly then said, "The man is a bastard." Zach bit down on his back teeth with enough force that his jaw cracked. "He was that way long before you were in his life. You didn't make him that way. You can't blame yourself for not seeing him for what he was. You're not alone in that. He's managed to fool the world. To hide who he really is." Zach pulled back and looked directly into her eyes. "You loved him. Sandoval used that love to hurt you. On top of being a bastard, he's a fool to abuse the precious gift you gave him." She raised a hand that trembled to his face. Zach caught that hand and pressed his mouth to her palm, kissing her there. "There's no way I can undo what he did to you. But I can show you how it should be when a man cares about a woman."

"Will you take me into the bedroom and show me now?"

Zach stared at her. He was hard and throbbing in an instant. Though his touch remained gentle, his hand fisted around hers. He wanted to touch her more than he wanted to see tomorrow. He wanted to taste her. Sweat broke out on his brow. "Sweetheart, I didn't mean I had to show you with sex. There are other ways a man shows a woman he cares. Everyday." He brushed a hand over her hair. "If and when you want to make love, we can get to that. We can get there. But there's no ticking clock. I'll wait to make love to you. We'll do this on your time. When you're ready."

That sounded long term. He'd never thought of one woman and the future. Was that where his head was going now, his head and his heart? Relationships weren't his thing. His childhood hadn't scarred him. He had the Turners to thank for that. But with his job, never knowing for sure if he'd come back from a mission, he'd never wanted a long term relationship. He never wanted to worry that if he didn't make it back, he'd be leaving someone who needed him on her own.

He'd never stayed with a woman longer than the brief downtime between missions. Sometimes not even that long. Keeping those times light and fun for both him and the woman had never been a problem. None of the women he'd been with had made him think beyond the short time he was with them. They'd certainly never inspired thoughts of relationships. But when he thought of Allison, he wasn't thinking of one or two nights.

"When you're ready," he repeated. "I want it to be perfect for you."

"It already is."

Her gaze had gone soft and she was looking up at him with trust. It made him want to hold her against him and give her the stars. His heart did a slow roll. He was still holding her face between his palms. He slid his thumb along her bottom lip then bent his mouth to hers.

Allison's hands came up and her fingers circled his wrists and gripped him. They were still in the living room. Zach lowered his hands from her face, and linking one hand with hers, tugged her toward the bedroom. She remained in place. Second thoughts? As much as he wanted this. Wanted her. He wouldn't rush her.

Zach turned to face her. "Allison?" he said gently.

She'd gone somewhere. He could see it, but she shook her head, clearly not wanting to elaborate.

"I'm fine," she said.

Was she? Now he hesitated, feeling nervous. Hell, he felt afraid. Had Sandoval also used sex to hurt her? Was that what her hesitation was about? She hadn't said and she didn't seem afraid at the prospect of having sex but Zach didn't know and the thought that making love with him could bring back to her that kind of pain gutted him. This time when she moved forward, Zach didn't.

His indecision must have shown on his face. Her own expression fell. Some of the color left her cheeks. She wrapped her arms around herself and bowed her head.

"It's fine if you don't want to. If you've changed your mind," she said quietly.

Not want to? Zach reached up and touched her cheek tenderly. "I want you more than I want my next breath." His erection throbbed, so badly did he want to be inside her. "But I don't want to rush this. I don't want to ruin this. Most of all I don't want to do anything to scare you or to hurt you. Nothing happens here that you don't want. All you have to do is tell me to stop."

She went into his arms again. Zach caught her to him.

"I want you too. I won't want you to stop." She spoke the words softly, but powerfully.

Zach kissed her. Allison returned his kiss and it was like fuel on his fire. When Zach broke away, his breath had grown rapid. He lowered his arms. Again he took one of her hands in his and resumed the walk to the bedroom.

Inside, Zach turned the lights on and closed the door. He was straining for her, but looking at her, at the vulnerability and the trust, made it easy to go slowly. Allison wasn't just another woman to get off with an orgasm and to get himself off. Everything in him was shouting: Mine. That she was his woman.

Slowly, he reached out and unbuttoned her blouse. Her hands covered his. For an instant she halted his movement, and gripped her blouse, holding the ends together in a gesture to cover herself.

He could guess what she was thinking. She was woefully thin. Her bones jutted out from her skin. Before she'd pulled the ends of her blouse together, he'd seen her ribs protrude. There was no doubt that Sandoval had done his best to starve her. Zach damned Sandoval to hell until he could send him there himself.

Zach had to fight to control the rage over that, not to let it show. Gently, he lowered one of her hands. With his eyes on hers, he brought it to his mouth and kissed it.

Allison's eyes dampened. "You make me feel beautiful."

"Not hard to do when you're looking at what I'm looking at."

He lowered her other arm to her side and removed her blouse. The bra gapped at her breasts that had suffered weight loss just like the rest of her and though her curves were diminished, she was a sexy, desirable woman just the same. Saliva pooled in Zach's mouth and all his blood went to his groin in a painful surge, so badly did he want to get his hands and his mouth on her.

He closed his eyes, calling upon all his restraint. "Give me a minute here."

But any hope he'd had to cool down was shattered when Allison wrapped her hands around his and placed them on her breasts.

* * *

Allison placed his hands on her. Large hands. Her hands on his barely covered them. Such incredibly strong hands yet they touched her and held her with a gentleness that belied the force she knew they were capable of. Force she knew he would never use to hurt her. Unlike Rafael. She swallowed hard and forced herself not to think about Rafael, to think only of Zach.

Zach opened his eyes. They now blazed. She could see he was trying to bank that blaze, to restrain himself, but she didn't want that. She wanted his passion—all of it—and she wanted to give him hers. The revelation was liberating.

She removed her hands from his and reached out to tug at his T-shirt. "I want to touch you too."

His gaze went hotter. "You can touch me as much as you'd like."

She raised the hem of his shirt. She couldn't reach all the way up to completely take off the top. Zach lifted his arms. The muscles in his shoulders, in his chest, bulged as he finished the job of removing the shirt himself. He tossed it onto the floor somewhere, now also flexing the muscles in the arm that bore his tattoo, then he was bare to her view.

Broad shoulders. Thick biceps. Lean abdomen taut and hard with muscles that were also clearly defined. And he'd thought her beautiful. The man was simply magnificent. She couldn't wait any longer to touch him.

She splayed her fingers on his chest. His skin was hot and beneath her hands, his muscles tensed and trembled. His heart sped up, beating hard against her palm. When she could tear her gaze away from his upper body, she looked up into his eyes. His gaze had intensified, darkened, filled with his desire for her. Looking at her, he had to be seeing that same desire for him reflected in her eyes.

She closed the distance between them completely so she was leaning against him. Slowly, tenderly, she kissed each bruise the brothers had caused that now marred his skin. His ribs had sustained the worst of it and she lavished attention there.

He sucked in a harsh, ragged breath. When he'd removed his shirt, he hadn't returned his hands to her body but had stood with his arms at his sides, allowing her the access she wanted to touch him, allowing her to dictate how they would proceed and at what pace. He was giving her what she needed and clearly, the slow pace she'd set was costing him. His jaw and his body were as taut as bow strings.

He closed his eyes now and his Adam's apple bobbed. "Do you know what you're doing to me, sweetheart?" His voice was thick, hoarse but without anger or censure.

She looked up at him. "I only know what you're doing to me."

She removed his belt then unzipped him. She worked the faded jeans and underwear down at the same time. His legs were strong, powerful. All those hard muscles visibly trembled at her touch and then his erection was revealed. She couldn't help but stare.

"Keep looking at me like that and this will be

over far too soon," he said.

Zach stepped out of his jeans and kicked them out of the way. He took her face in his hands. His mouth came down and glanced over hers. His touch was gentle as if she were the most precious thing to him He licked along her lips. She opened her mouth and he slid his tongue inside, stroking her, teasing her, leaving her breathless.

He broke away to gulp air. "I have no control with you."

His mouth came down on hers again and this time melded with hers. She had no control when it came to him either. She stroked her tongue against his and pressed her body against his so not even light could fit between them. She wanted more of him. All of him.

He seemed to want the same of her because his hands lowered from her face and began to move all over her as if he wanted to touch her everywhere and all at once. Against her lips he murmured, "I'm going to kiss and taste every inch of you."

Heat flooded her. She couldn't speak just then, could only nod.

He went down on one knee. She was still wearing her blouse. He eased it aside, baring her abdomen, and pressed his lips to the undersides of her breasts that were still in her bra. Holding her gently at the waist, he kissed a tender and thorough trail across her belly. He unsnapped her pants. Gently he lowered them, lavishing attention on the skin there as it was revealed to him, both front and back.

He came to an abrupt stop but Allison was

already too far gone to do more than acknowledge that he'd stopped. Then he continued on his way. He lowered her panties, baring her, then put his mouth on her and began a gentle, unhurried exploration of her with his tongue.

Allison's head fell back. With each slow stroke of his tongue he took her to a new height. She was quickly becoming consumed by need. Her legs quivered, no longer able to support her, and she clutched his shoulders.

Zach's hold on her waist tightened. He rose from the floor, lifting her with him so her feet no longer touched the carpeting but brushed against his knees. Allison gripped his shoulders. He was injured. Looking down at him, she feared the strain of carrying her would cause him hurt but he didn't seem to be in pain or even to strain as he walked with her to the bed.

He laid her carefully on the mattress then stood looming over her, staring down at her. His eyes were so hot, they scorched her. He came down beside her and his erection brushed her thigh, hot, thick and pulsing. Desire and anticipation surged through her but he made no move to enter her. Clearly, he wasn't ready for this to be over.

Slowly, he put his lips to her brow, her ear, her cheek, her lips. When she would have latched on to his mouth with her own, he moved on, kissing then licking a path down her neck, over her shoulders, to the top of one breast where he remained. He eased a finger to the front clasp and unhooked her bra then slid his mouth along her skin and used that skilled tongue on her nipple. He took his time stroking and sucking then moved on to focus on her other breast.

Allison clutched the bedspread. Her head thrashed against the pillow as her desire grew. Zach left her breasts, moved farther down her body and resumed tasting her with his tongue.

Again, he took his time, kissing her softly there one instant then swiping his tongue over her the next. Softly then harder his tongue played over her. Allison shivered. His touch left her quivering. She released the bedding and fisted her hands in his hair. One more touch and she was sure she'd go over the edge.

Zach stopped. Allison had been holding her breath and it blew out in a whoosh. Her next breath came hard and was loud in the quiet of the room. He was no longer touching her but she couldn't remain still. Instead, she was squirming on the mattress.

"I had more planned," Zach said. His voice was tense and strained. "But I can't wait. I have to have you now, Allison. You're killing me, sweetheart."

"I have to have you now too." Her words came out fast. She wanted him with a desperation she'd never known before.

Zach left her briefly and reached beneath the bed, pulling out the duffel bag he'd stashed beneath. She watched him roll on a condom, then he made his way up her body. His mouth came down on hers. His kiss was hard and he deepened it. Easing her legs apart, he nudged her, then no doubt finding her more than ready, he pushed slowly inside her.

His muscles bunched and rippled and his jaw clenched. He continued to give her more of himself and she moaned as he went deeper and filled her more each time he moved. When he was finally fully inside her, he went still.

"Okay?" he asked. "Tell me if you're not with me, sweetheart."

A line appeared on his forehead with his concern. Sweat popped on his brow and his biceps bulged with the strain he was obviously exerting to keep himself from moving.

Rather than respond with words, she lifted her head and fastened her mouth to his in a greedy kiss. Whatever leash Zach had on himself snapped when her mouth touched his. He fused his mouth to hers and thrust hard.

Allison could feel him swelling further, growing even larger within her. It appeared he couldn't get enough of her. She knew how he felt. She couldn't get enough of him either.

Their breathing was harsh and uneven, gasping. Zach moved faster, harder. Allison's breath caught and held, then her release overtook her and with her mouth still against his, she cried out his name. In the fog that enveloped her brain, she heard Zach's hoarse shout as he found his own completion.

Zach relaxed a bit on top of her, but caught himself before he could press her into the mattress and braced his weight on his arms. He was still deep inside her and stayed that way. His kisses became gentle, tender. "Okay?"

Her eyes had grown heavy, but she managed a

sleepy nod and a smile. "Oh, yeah."

He smiled and softly brushed her hair off her brow. "I need to get rid of the condom then I'll be back."

CHAPTER TWELVE

In the short time it took Zach to return to the bed, Allison had fallen asleep. Her chest rose and fell softly with her inhalations and exhalations. Her lips parted slightly in a soft sigh. He reached out and ran his finger down the side of her face and then because that wasn't enough he brushed his lips over her brow and lingered there.

Her skin felt cool. The bed covers had tangled during their lovemaking. Zach gently covered Allison without waking her then brought her against him and just watched her, asleep in his arms. He couldn't sleep himself. He couldn't get what he'd seen on her body out of his mind.

While he'd been making love to her, he'd come across marks on her skin that had halted him—burn marks. He didn't need to ask her what had made those marks. He knew about torture. He knew what would make those kinds of marks. Electricity. Sandoval had used electricity to torture her. Zach's chest tightened at what she'd endured.

He couldn't see the marks now, covered as she was, but he could still see them in his mind and his body went hot with a murderous rage. Allison moved against him. He forced himself to ease the muscles that had hardened and tensed so he wouldn't wake her. He was going to see Sandoval dead. There wasn't a corner in this world where that son of a bitch could hide from Zach. Zach would take that bastard apart with his bare hands.

Zach's body tensed again. Allison mumbled something in her sleep and stirred against him again. His attempt to control his fury wasn't working. She needed rest. In his current frame of mind, she wouldn't get that while he was in the bed with her. He pushed back the covers and left the bed.

* * *

Allison awoke alone in the bed. She pushed hair back from her face. What time was it? It had been after dinner when she'd come to bed with Zach. Now?

There wasn't a clock on the nightstand but she couldn't hear any sound coming from the rest of the house. She was betting it was late enough that the men who weren't on patrol had gone to sleep.

Where was Zach?

She rose onto an elbow to leave the bed and go in search of him when she saw him sitting in the arm chair in the corner. "Zach?"

"Sorry, sweetheart. I didn't mean to startle

you."

"You didn't." She blinked. "How long have you been sitting there?"

"A few hours. You've been in a deep sleep."

She sat up against the headboard. "I was dead to the world. I can't remember the last time I slept so soundly. I can't remember the last time I felt safe enough to sleep so soundly."

"You're going to feel safe again. You're going to *be* safe again." Zach's lips pulled tight forming two white slashes.

He left the chair and came to sit beside her on the bed. He leaned in and kissed her then cradled her nape and pressed her head to his chest. She closed her eyes, savoring being in his arms.

"What were you doing sitting there?" she asked.

"Couldn't sleep and I told you I wouldn't leave you in here to sleep alone, remember?"

She raised her head to look at him. "I remember. You said you'd be sleeping in here with me to protect me."

He nodded.

"You've been doing that, protecting me, since the day you took me back from Rafael. It took me time to see that."

"Doesn't matter now."

No, there was no point dwelling on the past. She'd put off telling him about Rafael long enough. Looking back, she realized she should have told Zach what she knew about Rafael when they were still at Brock's and she'd decided to leave there to go with Zach to this safe house. The more information Zach had, the better he'd be able to protect them both. And it wasn't just her life at risk now. If Rafael hurt Zach ... Goose bumps sprang on her arms with that fear.

She was still naked. Thinking of Rafael chilled her to the bone and she reached for the blanket to cover herself. "Rafael isn't going to give up and go away."

Zach wrapped an arm around her, warming her. "No, Sandoval is still out there, baby. Sooner or later we're going to have to engage him."

"Zach, there are things you need to know. Things I should have told you sooner."

"Tell me now, sweetheart."

"We can't continue to stay here."

Zach's gaze went razor sharp. "Why is that?"

"While we're here doing nothing, Rafael is making terrible plans. I don't know what his time frame is for implementing them, but we need to stop him now."

Zach's eyes went as hard as flint. He clasped her shoulders, his fingers gently stroking the skin there. "Why don't you tell me what you know?"

His calm voice was reassuring as was his gentle but firm hold, telling her as surely as words that she was no longer alone in this.

"Rafael has been lying," she said.

Zach's mouth firmed. "You said that earlier. What specifically is he lying about?"

"All his talk about democratizing his country and mending relations with the U.S. and the rest of the world is bullshit. He's built a nuclear weapon."

* * *

She sounded certain. Zach bent and looked directly into her eyes. "How do you know this?"

She lowered her eyes from his and linked her fingers. She'd wound them so tightly the tips whitened. Zach gently eased them apart and linked her fingers with his.

"We didn't have a honeymoon," she began. "Rafael said he had to return to his country as soon as we were married. That he'd been away too long and his people needed him. Things between Rafael and me changed as soon as we boarded his plane to South America. So fast it was as if a switch had been flipped and he became a different man. He acted as if he couldn't stomach the sight of me. I didn't know what brought about the change.

"I was upset. I wanted to talk to him right away, to find out what was wrong but we were never alone. His staff and personal guards were always around. I decided I'd talk to him as soon as we reached his house, but I didn't need to. When we arrived at his home, he told me the way things were and the way things were going to be. He told me straight out that he hated me. That he'd always hated me. He said he'd only married me because he wanted an American wife. He'd never wanted me for *me*. Any woman would have served as well as long as she was American.

"He intended to parade her—me—to the world to show how modern he was, to gain acceptance and to ease him into negotiations for American aid. All he wanted was money and the power that money would bring him. You were right, he put on an act to fool the world and he'd done the same thing with me to fool me into marrying him.

"I was shocked. Devastated. But I was also angry. My marriage was not real. I had too much respect for myself to stay with a man who didn't want me. I was certainly not going to let him use me. I told him all that. We'd been traveling from the moment we were married. We hadn't consummated the marriage. I told him I would get a divorce or in this case an annulment."

Zach tensed. "What did he do then?"

"He told me I wouldn't need a divorce or an annulment because soon I'd be dead." She squeezed her eyes tightly and swallowed several times before opening them again. "I was terrified. I didn't know when he intended to kill me. All I knew was I had to get away. I realized then that Rafael had my passport. He had my money. I'd closed my bank accounts in the States and had no accounts in Rafael's country. My only chance was to find a way to get to the American Consulate and from there get in touch with my family to send me the documents and the money I needed to get out of South America.

"I was given a sparse, isolated bedroom on a floor above his. I waited until night then put my bathrobe on to hide my clothes in case I encountered Rafael and left my room. Looking back on my plan to just walk out of his house, I can see how naive it was. His home resembled what I thought a military compound was like. There were guards patrolling the grounds and towers and even inside the house. I don't know how I expected to be able to slip away. I was terrified and desperate enough to try and think I had a chance.

"Downstairs, in the hall, I saw a man. I knew him. He was one of the men who worked for Rafael, one of Rafael's trusted people who'd traveled with us on the plane. The man—Javier—was alone and he had a gun in his hand. The way he looked at me, I was terrified he was going to shoot me. But he didn't. Instead, he was on me before I could get away. He told me I had to get out of there. He told me I didn't know the kind of man my husband was. That I wasn't safe with Rafael. It struck me that Javier no longer had a South American accent. He sounded American.

"Before I could say anything to Javier, Rafael and several of his men came running down the hall. The men were all heavily armed. They grabbed Javier—or whatever his name was—and disarmed him. As they took hold of him, Javier stumbled and fell into me. Rafael began shouting questions at Javier, accusations. He called Javier a spy. Rafael was furious, out of control. When Javier refused to answer, Rafael shot him in the face."

Allison paled and Zach tightened his grip on her hand and wrapped his other arm around her.

"Rafael started shouting those same questions at me—something about who was I working for," Allison went on. "Did I think I'd get away with spying on him? He accused me of setting him up not the other way around." Allison shook her head. "Crazy talk, but then I'd just seen Rafael shoot a man. I'd learned my marriage was a nightmare and my husband intended to kill me."

Her voice cracked. "It couldn't get any crazier. I was in shock, I guess. I only heard some of what he was yelling and of course I didn't know what he was talking about. I told him that. That I'd only happened to come across Javier now.

"Rafael didn't believe me. He became even more enraged. He put the gun to my face. I thought he was going to kill me too. I could see in his face that he wanted to." Allison's pulse pounded visibly at her throat. "At the last second, he didn't. He had his men take me to the lower level of the house." She bowed her head. Her voice thinned to a hoarse whisper. "I don't know how long I was down there but one day I was taken out and returned to my bedroom."

There was something she'd left out. Zach frowned but before he could ask her, she went on.

"Shortly after, Rafael came into my room. He told me we were going to the U.S. on a diplomatic visit. That the only reason he'd kept me alive—the only reason he'd married me—was to accompany him on this trip. I knew then he would kill me after the trip was over.

"I was in a panic after he left. I knocked my bathrobe off its hook and a small memory card fell out of the pocket. I remembered Javier had stumbled into me in the hall and I realized he must have dropped the card into my pocket that night in the hall. He'd known he was caught and hadn't wanted Rafael to find it on him."

"What was on the card, sweetheart?"

"Information and Rafael—Rafael talking with other men about a nuclear weapon he'd developed that was ready to be implemented. Rafael called it *his* weapon and said there wasn't a weapon to equal it."

She was shaking now. Zach pressed his lips to her brow. "What did you do?"

"If that weapon were used, so many people would die. I couldn't let him do that. I had to tell someone. I didn't know who to tell. I hid the card. I had to get that information to someone in the U.S. The media, I thought, but I didn't know how to get the card past Rafael to take it with me when we left his country. The next day a seamstress arrived to fit me for the clothing Rafael wanted me to wear while we were on the trip. One of the items was a gown Rafael selected for me to wear on his last night in the U.S. at a gala to be held in his honor. After the seamstress was finished with me and wouldn't be returning, I sewed the card into the hem of that gown and I decided I'd find a way to leave Rafael that night of the gala. I planned to take the card to the media. That's where I was headed when you stopped me.

"If I didn't get away during the gala, it would be too late. He was taking me back to South America the morning after. If he took me back, he'd kill me and no one would know the truth about him and what he was planning until it was too late." Her voice dropped. "I couldn't let him take me back there." She shuddered.

She stopped speaking and Zach believed that time was replaying in her mind. Her eyes dimmed. Zach felt a punch to the gut at the bleakness he saw there. "Allison, tell me the rest.

What are you leaving out?"

Her face lost its color. Her breathing grew harsh and ragged. Whatever she was thinking of was tearing her up inside. Zach had gotten what he needed to know from her about Sandoval and about her evidence. Zach didn't believe there was anything more she could tell him about the nuke. No, this was something else. His gut was burning with it. He didn't need to press her further but he had to know what she was still holding back. Could not *not* know. "What did Sandoval do when he took you to the lower level of his compound?"

"You have all the information you need. That's all there is."

Zach was holding her, felt her tug back, trying to leave. He continued to hold her. Where her eyes had been bleak an instant earlier, they now flashed. He ignored the anger in her tone but he couldn't ignore the pain. "That isn't all there is," he said gently. "What happened with Sandoval?"

"The rest doesn't matter. It has nothing to do with his plans."

"The hell it doesn't matter." The agony in her eyes was almost his undoing. "Allison, tell me what happened."

He could see her struggle to comply, her indecision, her wariness. He saw her yearning. She wanted to tell him, but she held herself back. She wanted someone to share whatever was shredding her. She wanted someone to lean on. It struck him like a gale force wind how much he wanted her to lean on him. "Baby, tell me."

Her eyes filled then overflowed. Tears slid

down her cheeks. "He put me in a—a cell." Her voice came choked with tears. "He began to interrogate me. He thought I was working with Javier. That I was spying on him and giving Javier information. He had one of his men hold me while the other beat me and when that wasn't enough, he used electricity. But beatings and electricity left marks. He didn't want that. He didn't want any signs of abuse before our trip. Rafael told me he'd planned on killing me anyway when he got what he wanted from the U.S. That I'd never been more than a means to that end. He'd planned to kill me and make it look like an accident, but now, now he would tell the world that I'd become mentally ill and killed myself. And he began the injections.

"There was no light in the cell. Rafael left me in the dark all the time. His voice or a voice I didn't recognize spoke out of the darkness. Over and over I was told that I'd lost my mind. That I was ... insane."

Allison had drawn in tight and wrapped her arms around herself as if to shield herself. She was trembling in his arms, her strength depleted, her spirit crushed. Every muscle in Zach's body tensed with rage. Food deprivation. Beatings. Electrical torture. Drugs. He'd known some of what that son of a bitch had done to her but not all of it. He hadn't realized how much it would hurt him to know it all.

Of all the things Sandoval had done to Allison, Zach could see that Sandoval's relentless attack on her sanity came closest to breaking her. Zach felt fury he'd never known before. It was a living breathing thing within him. He had to get it under control. Sandoval, the one his rage was directed at, wasn't here. Allison was and she looked ... destroyed.

Her tears soaked his bare chest. She burrowed into him as if she could crawl inside him. That would have suited him fine. He would stand between her and whatever would hurt her. God help Sandoval if he tried to take her from Zach.

He didn't have the words to make this right. What words could possibly make any of what happened to her right? But he had to try. He couldn't bear to see her like this with her insides bleeding.

He nudged her chin up so she could look no where but at him. "If that bastard were here now, I would gut him." Zach's body primed with the urge to do just that. "But that won't turn the clock back so none of what he did to you ever happened." Zach reached up and brushed the tears on her cheeks with his thumbs. "I'm sorry for all he did to you. I can't tell you how sorry." Zach's heart felt squeezed in a vise. "I'm here for you, sweetheart. I will do anything to get you through this. I will do anything to make this better for you."

She stared into his eyes, her own drenched in tears. "You've done so much. You can't know how much."

As far as Zach was concerned, he hadn't done the one thing he needed to do. He hadn't killed Sandoval. Yet.

CHAPTER THIRTEEN

Allison remained in his arms, neither of them speaking as the night wore on. The wind picked up. Zach could hear it rattle the windows.

Eventually, she slept. But it was exhausted sleep, not relaxed sleep. Zach could feel the tension in her. He drew the covers over them both and laid down on the bed with her still in his arms.

He couldn't sleep. The horrors she'd described played over in his mind. He was awake to see the sunrise and to hear her stomach growl. Allison opened her eyes, but seemed okay to ignore her hunger. No doubt a result of the times with Sandoval when she'd had to. Zach wouldn't. He pressed his lips to her hair in a long kiss. "Let's see what's in the kitchen."

* * *

Allison awoke to the feel of Zach's lips

tenderly caressing hers.

"Morning, sweetheart," he said.

He was leaning over her. She looked up at him. "Morning."

Was it still morning? She caught a glimpse of Zach's wrist watch. Just barely.

Sometime after dawn, after they'd had the last of the lasagna, Zach had carried her back to bed. He'd gone on holding her and touching her. He'd made long, slow, tender love to her again, letting her know with his body that he was with her, that she wasn't alone. She closed her eyes against a rush of tears, recalling his unending patience, giving and caring.

After, he'd drawn them a bath. In the warm, soapy water, Zach's arms had been like steel bands around her, holding her against his chest, giving her comfort she'd never thought to feel.

At some point, her eyelids drooped. She never felt him lift her from the tub and place her in the bed.

She'd told him of that time in the cell. Laid bare the thoughts and emotions that still felt like open wounds. She hadn't thought she'd be able to open up about that time with anyone, ever. But Zach wasn't just anyone ...

He kissed her again now. The touch of his lips, so gentle, so tender, had tears burning her throat. She made a small sound.

Zach pulled back and looked down at her. "Okay?"

A line appeared between his brows with his concern. How could she explain to him just what his concern meant to her? What being here with him meant to her?

She smoothed that line on his brow softly with her fingertips and didn't try to put into words what she was feeling. Instead, she just nodded.

He went on watching her. After a time, he clasped her hand where it still stroked his brow and brought it to his lips, kissing the backs of her fingers.

He kept her hand in his and returned his mouth to hers. He kept the pressure easy, light, playful. She wanted to be able to be playful with him. She wanted to put Rafael and all the pain behind her and take joy in this moment.

Zach continued to coax her. She closed her eyes, pushing aside everything in her mind but him. When his kiss brought on a delicious shiver, she clutched his neck and licked a slow line across his mouth.

He hissed a long breath. His hands slid down her back and cupped her bottom. He nuzzled her neck, gently pushing aside her hair, then put his lips to the soft skin behind her ear. It had to be one of her sweet spots. Definitely an erogenous zone for her. As he devoted attention to that single spot, he drove her deliciously higher.

He licked that tender area. Slowly. Unhurried. Allison's body rose up off the bed. Zach had yet to shave and his stubble brushed lightly across her skin with each swipe of his tongue.

She reached down and grasped his erection. Thick and pulsing it kicked in her tight grip. Zach closed his eyes, gritted his teeth through another long hiss of breath.

She wanted all of him. She slid out from under

him. She flattened her palms on his hard chest and pushed him onto his back on the mattress. She bent over him, lowering her head to his erection. Her fair fell onto his ridged abdomen and swept across his skin. His muscles bunched and quivered.

As he'd done with her, she swept her tongue over him in long slow laps. Down then up, then down again. Zach shut his eyes and his jaw tightened. She swirled her tongue across the broad tip of his erection then took him deep. Zach groaned.

"Enough, sweetheart. You're so beautiful and I'm not ready for this to be over."

He hooked her beneath her arms and lifted her, placing her gently on her back on the mattress. He blew out a long breath then another. When he had himself under control, he smiled a wolf's smile, then hot and wet his mouth closed over her breast. She arched toward him and let out a small hiss of her own at the exquisite sensation.

"Like that, do you?" His eyes glinted.

He knew well that she did. She smiled at his teasing. "I think you know everything I like."

"Let's test that theory."

He kissed his way down her body. When he reached her sides, he kissed her ribs, tickling her in the process. Allison laughed.

He continued to kiss her sides. Finally, she couldn't take any more tickling. "Okay. Okay. No more." Her voice rang with laughter.

Zach's body shook with laughter of his own. He reached under the bed and an instant later sheathed himself with a condom. He raised himself so he was again above her. Grinning, he kissed the tip of her nose then gently probed her entrance, stretching her and awakening every nerve ending.

"How about this?" he said. "Like this?"

Allison sucked in a breath. "Yes." Her eyelids fluttered with sensation that threatened to overwhelm her. "Oh, yes, more of that."

He eased forward in a single small thrust. Allison dug her heels into the mattress.

"That enough?" he asked.

She didn't know how he was still able to tease when he was so obviously straining for release. She could hear it in his voice that had lowered and gone raspy and she could feel him inside her, so engorged now, he stretched her inner walls so she thought she couldn't stretch any more. Having him filling her that completely had her trembling with need.

Her fingers dug into his nape but she tossed back. "Not quite."

"No, huh?"

His laughter didn't come as easily as it had a moment earlier, but he stayed his course. In and out. He nudged her then withdrew, rocking her with slow thrusts that he kept from penetrating her too deeply. Her body had awakened to his and even those small, shallow movements took her to the brink.

He kept up that pace. Kept her on the very edge. Wanting. Craving. Needing. But she wasn't alone. She felt him shudder with the control he was exerting.

Then all traces of teasing left him. Zach kissed her open-mouthed, his tongue delving deep, and sank all the way inside her. He set the same rhythm with his tongue as he did with his thrusts. Allison pushed against him, matching him stroke for stroke. Harder. Deeper. Faster. He moved at a pace that sent her desire soaring. She gasped, unable to breathe. Her vision filled with light then she cried out, into his mouth, from a pleasure that went on and on. Zach's hoarse cry of release followed.

Zach's breathing was fast and loud. Or maybe that was her breathing?

Their mouths were still touching and he kissed her slowly now and with a tenderness that squeezed her heart.

They stayed like that, with their bodies joined and their mouths moving softly against each other, while their breathing and their heart rates returned to their normal rhythms.

Eventually Zach moved his head and spoke softly into her ear. "You know, I never did get to that ice cream."

She looked up at him. Her lips curved in a smile. "Last I saw, there was plenty of it in the freezer."

Zach brushed one knuckle softly down her cheek. "How about we go get some?"

* * *

Allison was with Briggs who was showing her the fine points of making perfect French Toast for what was going to turn out to be breakfast in the afternoon. Zach turned his attention elsewhere.

Sandoval had to be stopped. As long as that nuke was in his hands, lives would be at risk. And the one life that Zach could not live without would be at risk—Allison. Not only was she at risk if that son of a bitch used the weapon, but until Sandoval was disarmed, he would continue to hunt Allison to prevent her from telling what she knew about the nuke. It was time to end this. Zach called John. John answered his secure line on the first ring.

"Zach?"

"Yeah."

"What's going on? What have you found out since we last talked?"

"That you were right. Sandoval's got a nuke the likes of which we've never seen before. He's not developing it, John. It's good to go."

"Fuck. Any idea where he's stashed this nuke?"

"No, but I know where I can find that information. At his compound. I'm going after it."

"How do you know it's there?" John asked.

"I have Allison Sandoval with me."

"Allison Sandoval? That why you wanted the Intel on Rafael Sandoval?"

"Yeah. She knows about the nuke. That's why Sandoval wants to find her."

John blew out a breath. "I can send our agents down there with you. Go with you myself. Give you back up."

"I want to wait on that. Sandoval will be on the look out for your people. John, he learned of the agent you had down there. I have confirmation on that."

"From whom?"

"Allison. Your agent made contact with her. She saw Sandoval shoot him dead."

John was quiet for a moment then asked, "How do you want to do this?"

"Morse wants Allison as much as Sandoval. I don't want you to go down to South America with me. I need you to be here, to keep her safe for me."

"Okay," John said. "Tell me what you have in mind."

"We'll need to file a flight plan to South America, though we'll give a different destination than Sandoval's country. Before we set on that course, we'll make an off-the-books stop at Danvers County Airstrip." Danvers County was a short jaunt from John. "I need you to meet me there to get Allison. I want to leave her with you and Eve. Once I know Allison is safe with you, my people and I will continue on to Sandoval's compound."

"When do you want to do this?"

"I need a few days to put this together. I'll be back in touch once I have."

"I'll wait for your call."

"John," Zach's voice was tense, "just you at the airstrip. I can't risk this leaking and Morse or Sandoval finding out where Allison is."

"Just me. I'll take care of her for you."

Zach knew that to be the truth. He ended the call with John. Now to speak with Allison.

She was still in the kitchen with Briggs. Zach heard Briggs speaking as he approached.

"Now this recipe has been passed down from generation to generation in my mother's family. I have to swear you to secrecy." Briggs gave her a conspiratorial smile and crooked his baby finger in a pinkie swear.

Allison returned his smile and hooked her much smaller finger to his. "I swear. Now tell all."

She looked more at ease than Zach had ever seen her. He hated that he was about to end that.

Briggs's gaze left hers and connected with Zach's. Allison turned.

"Briggs, can you give us a minute?" Zach asked.

Briggs nodded. "Sure thing."

"This better be important, Zach, for you to interrupt us," Allison said. "Briggs was about to divulge the ingredients on the recipe for his grandmother's French Toast." She was grinning but Zach didn't return her smile and her smile faltered. "What is it? What's happened?"

"I've made arrangements for you to stay elsewhere."

"Why am I not going to continue staying with you?"

He took one of her hands loosely in his. "We need the information on the nuke and I need you to be safe. I'm going after that information."

She lost some of the color in her face but firmed her lips. "What you want is back in South America. I'll come with you. You haven't seen Rafael's compound. I have."

Zach gave her the full force of his stare. "Not going to happen. What you're going to do is stay where you'll be safe. My people and I will take care of this."

"You and these men here?" Two red spots appeared on Allison's cheeks. Her voice vibrated with desperation. "A handful of men against Rafael's army isn't enough."

Her hand was now ice cold in his. Zach brushed his thumb across the backs of her fingers. "It won't be just me and the men I have here, sweetheart. Three more of my men will meet us at the airstrip. They're on leave. I'll call them back. I'll call in my other two teams as well. They'll meet us in South America. We'll have more than enough manpower."

Allison's brows drew together and she bit into her lower lip. "Why does it have to be you and your people? The CIA must want Rafael. You said your CIA contact wants to talk to me." She shivered then straightened her shoulders. "I'll speak with him." She squeezed Zach's hand. Hers was trembling. "Leave Rafael to them. Let them stop him."

It was a testament to how afraid she was for him that she would talk to Morse. "This is what I do, baby. And with Sandoval," Zach's voice lowered, became lethal, "this is personal. I will make sure he can't ever hurt you again."

"And what about you?" Her mouth trembled. "You don't know Rafael and if he knows you've helped me, he'll target you specifically. He will hurt you because of me. I can't stand by and let him hurt you."

Zach broke into a sweat thinking of her vulnerable to Sandoval. "If you really want to help me, then you'll do as I ask you and stay where I know you'll be safe." Zach's eyes bore into hers. "The thought of you back with Sandoval, knowing you're hurt, in pain, terrifies me. Allison, I need to know you're safe. There is nothing in this world that matters more to me than that. There is nothing in this world that matters more to me than you. I love you. You are everything to me."

Zach stared into her eyes for a long moment then leaned down to her. He moved his mouth over hers as if it had been months instead of moments since he'd last kissed her. He wasn't the only one doing the kissing, wasn't the only one that held her in a death-grip. Allison was holding him to her just as fiercely, her fingers digging into his waist.

When she pulled back, her eyes were damp with tears. "Do you think that's any different for me?"

He lowered his head until his brow touched hers. "Then you know where I'm coming from. Do this for me, baby."

He must have conveyed the stark fear he felt at the thought of her in danger because she nodded. "I love you, Zach. I don't want to make this harder for you. I'll go where you want. Promise me that you'll keep yourself safe. You're everything to me too."

He leaned in and kissed her again. Against her lips, he gave her his promise. "Nothing in this world will keep me from coming back to you."

A shudder went through her then she asked softly, "You haven't said where I'll be going?"

Zach loosened his hold on her and looked

down at her. "You'll be staying with John Burke. He's family, John and his wife, Eve. John is with the CIA. Eve works for John." At her widened eyes, Zach added, "Listen to me, sweetheart. John is not working with the CIA contact who's now looking for you. I trust John with my life. He isn't doing the job here. This isn't about the job. This is about family. He would never give you up. He will protect you with his life. If I didn't know that, I wouldn't leave you with him."

She pressed tight to him again. "I trust you. I'll go with John. I'm not changing my mind. I don't want you to worry about me. I want you to be focused on Rafael. When do I go?"

"Just as soon as I can put this together."

Zach felt her stiffen in fear and just as quickly work to control it. He hated that he was going to be forced to leave her, but he had no choice. She would never be safe until Sandoval was out of her life and unable to hurt her. Zach drew back and nudged her chin up. He kissed her long and deeply. Briggs poked his head around the corner.

"First batch of French Toast is on the table," Briggs called out.

Zach kissed her a moment longer then said, "Let's get you fed."

CHAPTER FOURTEEN

Four days later, Chase drove Zach's SUV onto the Corrigan airstrip where the company planes were hangared. One of them was already on the runway ready for the flight. Allison's breathing picked up. She made an effort to regulate it. She'd known the time at the safe house couldn't last forever, that the reprieve had to come to an end. But knowing that didn't stop the fear that threatened to consume her at being separated from Zach. She had no way of knowing what the next hours would bring. Zach had told her she was everything to him, but he'd become everything to her and she was terrified that she would lose him and all they had together.

Her hand was in Zach's, engulfed by his much larger one. As if he sensed her thoughts and fears, he gave her a squeeze. She had to do better to hide her fear. He couldn't be worried about her. He needed to be clear-headed. She squeezed Zach's hand in return, this time to reassure him.

Chase parked beside a truck that held the three men Zach had told her were meeting them here then cut the engine. Zach nodded to the men then turned to her.

"Stay behind me at all times," he said.

"Okay."

"Ready?"

As much as she would ever be. She nodded.

Zach got out of the vehicle. Chase, Hamilton and Briggs got out next and took up positions on either side of Zach. He reached back inside the SUV for Allison. She placed her hand in his and he slowly drew her out onto the tarmac.

The four large men formed a wall, blocking her view of anything but them. She heard rather than saw the doors to the other vehicle being opened then closed and presumed those men had left their truck as well.

Zach took up the lead, keeping her behind him, and the other men moved to shield her on her sides and back. The muscles in Zach's back and shoulders were tense and he had one hand on the gun holstered at his shoulder.

Without turning around, he said to his men, "Move out."

Zach's tension didn't ease as they stepped away from his SUV. If anything, Allison could see his body become more rigid and his head didn't cease its movement as he continuously scanned their surroundings.

"Something's off," Zach said under his breath and came to a halt.

Chase's hand tightened on his weapon. "What do you see?"

Before Zach could reply, the hatch to the plane opened and a man stepped onto the platform.

Zach moved with lightning speed, diving behind the SUV, taking Allison with him.

Before Allison could blink, he'd pushed her to the ground, covering her with his body, and his gun was in his hand.

Zach's other men had also taken cover behind the two vehicles, their own guns at the ready. Two men braced assault rifles at their shoulders and squinted through the scopes.

"You're not taking her, Westwood," Zach shouted, his voice hard.

Allison went still. Of course this had to be about her, but who was this man named Westwood? One of Rafael's men? Whoever Westwood was, he was known to Zach.

The man at the plane—Westwood—shook his head slowly and smiled. "You know I have to, Zach. My men have you surrounded. We can pick you off one by one."

To illustrate his point, a bullet blew out a headlight on the truck driven by Zach's other men. Hamilton had taken cover behind that vehicle and the bullet struck mere inches away from Hamilton's head. Zach's hand plopped onto Allison's head, pushing her face flat to the ground and he dropped on top of her so completely, he blocked all daylight.

Zach was breathing hard. Allison could feel the rage coming off him. She heard another gun shot. The sound was deeper, made by a rifle.

"I can play that game as well, Westwood," Zach called out. "Make this a real pissing contest.

Shoot holes in you and your men. I can guarantee none of you will make it out of here alive."

"You won't be walking out of here, either, Corrigan." Westwood's tone was tight and angry now. Gone was the calm manner. "Morse doesn't want her dead but he didn't say anything about not taking you out."

Morse. Zach's CIA contact. Zach had gone against Morse and not delivered her. Morse hadn't told his people not to kill Zach. Allison's heart rate felt as if it tripled. She pushed against Zach. "Let me up. Zach, please, you have to let me up." Zach didn't budge. Allison pushed harder. "I can't let you all be killed because of me."

"You let us worry about that," Zach said.

Gunfire erupted all around them. Zach and his men returned fire. Allison's breathing accelerated. She didn't doubt Zach and his teams' abilities, but the longer this went on, the greater the chance of one or more of them being hurt or killed.

Zach shifted position, aimed, then fired another several rounds. When Zach moved, Allison took the opportunity to scoot out from underneath him. One of Zach's men, who'd arrived in the other vehicle, stuck his head up from behind the hood to take better aim and fell back with a grunt then a deep groan. The man had been shot.

Zach shouted, "Braddock, do you have him?"

The instant Braddock revealed himself, a spate of gunfire filled the air. Braddock, too, was shot. Blood flowed from his chest.

Allison shouted. "Stop! Please!"

She was screaming to be heard above the gunfire. The shots ceased. Before Zach or anyone could stop her, she ran out from behind Zach's SUV.

"I'll go with you, Westwood," Allison called out, her voice breaking, "if you give me your word that Zach and his men won't be hurt anymore. That you'll let the men get the medical attention they need. Let them leave."

"Allison, what are you doing? No!" Zach's voice was tense and angry. "Get back here!"

She was terrified he would make a grab for her and in so doing, come out of hiding where Westwood and his people would shoot him. Panic rose within her. She walked quickly, deeper onto the tarmac. "Zach, these people don't want to hurt me, but they don't care if they kill all of you. I can't let them do that."

"She's right, Corrigan," Westwood called back. "We only want to talk to her. You know where she'll be. Take it up with Morse."

"I don't trust Morse, Westwood." Zach's tone dripped acid. "Allison, don't trust Westwood. Turn around and walk back to me."

Zach's voice had gone tight and strained when he'd addressed her. She could hear his fear for her. She was terrified herself at going with Westwood to meet Morse. She didn't really know what Morse's intentions toward her were. She didn't believe she would be killed, but she only had Westwood's word that she wouldn't be harmed. She summoned her courage. She'd been hurt by the best—Rafael—and she'd lived through it. If she could survive that, she could survive anything. Anything but if Zach were killed. Her heart skipped a beat then beat twice as fast. She would not let that happen.

She stared straight at Westwood and infused as much steel into her voice as she was able. "Your word, Westwood, that you'll allow Zach and his people to leave here. I need to hear it now. Zach's men need medical help."

"Allison, don't do this." Zach's voice sounded tortured.

Allison broke eye contact with Westwood and faced Zach. "I have to. I can't let any of you be killed because of me. And what will you all have died for anyway? Once he's killed all of you, he'll take me with him just the same."

She saw the truth of her words in Zach's eyes, along with the anger, the despair and the futility.

Westwood inclined his head in what could have been taken as a gallant gesture. "You have my word, Mrs. Sandoval. I have no reason to kill Zach or any of his people if you cooperate. Tell me how you want to do this."

She reluctantly pulled her gaze from Zach. "You let Zach and his men drive out of here and then, when it's just the two of us, Westwood, I'll come to you."

"Corrigan," Westwood said, "you're all free to go. Load up your wounded and drive out of here. Remember, our guns will be on you at all times."

Zach gave the order to his men. "Get Braddock and McMurtry in the trucks. Haul ass out of here." While his people were complying, Zach said, "Take me with you, Westwood. Like you said, I'll be on my way to Morse anyway."

Westwood gave a short humorless laugh. "You think I have a death wish? I know you'll kill me as soon as you get near me. Not going to happen. You'll have to find your own way to Morse."

Allison didn't doubt Zach would kill Westwood. The other man wasn't fool enough to let Zach get close. Zach made no move to leave, but held his position.

"Zach, go!" Allison's voice cracked. She had to know he was safe.

Zach's men drove away, but he remained behind with his weapon thrown to the ground. No. *No.* Allison wanted him gone where she knew he was no longer a target for Westwood and his men. The only way to remove that threat was to follow through on her promise. And she had to make sure Zach didn't do anything to provoke Westwood. She could all but feel Zach's body straining toward her with intent to prevent Westwood from taking her.

She turned to Zach. "Don't do anything. Westwood and his people are expecting you to make a move against them. Please don't make me watch you die." Tears blurred her view of him. "I can survive anything but that."

His face, that was tight with rage, now filled with pain and grief.

As she walked to Westwood, who now stood behind the open door of a black truck, she felt Zach's gaze burning into her. When she reached Westwood, she turned and looked back at Zach.

The expression in his eyes was of agony. "I'll come for you, Allison. I'll be with you soon."

Allison's throat closed and for a moment she couldn't speak. "I'm counting on that."

Then Westwood gave her a little push into the vehicle and drove them away.

CHAPTER FIFTEEN

Before Westwood left, he had one of his men shoot out all four tires on Zach's SUV. Zach had never felt more helpless in his life. Rage seethed in him, but above that, was fear, despair and self-directed anger. Zach could figure how Morse found out about the flight to South America. The flight plan they'd had to file. But why would Morse have been watching for one of Zach's people to file a flight plan? It made no sense. Morse would have had to know that Allison was with Zach. How had Morse found out that Allison was even with him?

Zach retrieved his weapon from the ground. While he changed one tire for the spare, he called Chase. When Chase responded Zach asked, "What's the status of Braddock and McMurtry?"

"They're alive."

Chase's grim tone told Zach that Braddock and McMurtry were in bad shape. Zach closed his eyes, feeling the pain for his men. "What's your

ETA at Blake County General?"

"Ten minutes or so."

To be that close, Briggs, who was driving, had to be breaking all speed limits. "I'll be there as soon as I can." Zach had never not been with one of his people who'd been injured. It was a code he lived by. They never left a man behind and they stayed with that injured man until he was treated and recovered or laid to rest. But this time, Zach couldn't be with Braddock and McMurtry. He had to get to Allison. "I'm going after Allison."

"I'll meet you at Morse's," Chase said.

"Negative. Stay with Braddock and McMurtry."

Zach ended the call. Pushing the disabled SUV to its limits, he drove away from the airfield.

* * *

When Zach reached the CIA office, Chase was waiting by the front door. He pushed off the brick at Zach's approach.

Zach's lip curled in an outward display of the anger he was feeling. "You hard of hearing all of a sudden? I told you to stay with McMurtry and Braddock. We stay with our team."

Chase's expression remained steady. "Braddock and McMurtry are in surgery. There isn't anything I can do for them right now and they'd have kicked my ass to the curb themselves. You're our team as well and right now you need me. By the look on your face, I'm going to be the only thing to keep you from killing Morse in the next few minutes."

Zach couldn't deny that. "Let's get this done."

Zach pushed through the double doors to the building that housed the CIA offices. He had no doubt he was expected. Westwood would have relayed Zach's message to Morse.

Zach and Chase were escorted to Morse's office right away and Zach got right to the point. "I want Allison. Now."

Morse sat behind his desk, a coffee mug in one hand. He took a long swallow before setting the cup slowly and deliberately back on the desk top. "Why was she with you?"

Zach gave Morse a hard look. "How did you find out Allison *was* with me?"

"I didn't. I got lucky. When you filed the flight plan for South America, though it wasn't to Sandoval's country, I had to make sure that wasn't where you were going. That Sandoval hadn't hired you. I couldn't let you do a job for Sandoval now. I sent Westwood to the airstrip to find out what was going on and to bring you in if necessary. Westwood saw you and your people exit your vehicle with Allison Sandoval and called me. I told him to bring her instead."

Zach's eyes narrowed. His voice went dangerously low. "What do you mean you couldn't let me do a job for Sandoval now? What did you do? Where is Allison?"

The unmistakable roar of an airplane engine penetrated the room. Morse's gaze lifted to the window.

The CIA office had a private airstrip on the grounds. Even as Zach ran to the door, with Chase on his heels intent on making it to the airstrip, the roar began to fade and Zach knew it was too late, the plane was in the air.

Zach lunged for Morse, seizing him by the throat. "You son of a bitch! What did you do?" Zach knocked over the chair Morse was sitting in, sending Morse to the floor in a heap. Zach hit the floor as well. "Where is she? Answer me you bastard!" Zach shook Morse like a rag doll.

The door to Morse's office burst open. A woman screamed then dashed back out. In the red haze clouding his brain, Zach figured he had about two minutes before the woman summoned help and men stormed Morse's office to try to haul Zach off their boss. Good luck to them with that.

"Where. Is. She." Zach asked the question from between clenched teeth.

Morse coughed and Zach eased his hold on Morse's throat fractionally, only enough to let Morse draw enough air to answer the question. Morse coughed again.

"Where?" Zach roared.

"With Sandoval. Sandoval wants his wife back. Whatever their marital differences, that's for them to work out."

Zach's nostrils flared. "You bastard. Do you even know what he did to her? What he'll do to her now. How he'll make her suffer for leaving him."

Zach's fury reached boiling point. He let loose, driving his fist into Morse's face. The crunch of bone, Morse's cry of pain, and the blood that ran from Morse's broken nose and front tooth gave Zach no satisfaction. None of that brought

Allison back to him.

He was breathing hard in a combination of desperation and fear. "Marital differences? You sanctimonious son of a bitch. He gave her drugs that pushed her to the edge of her sanity. He tortured her with electric shock. She went through hell and now because of you she's back with Sandoval where he can torture her all over again."

Chase wrapped both arms around Zach in an attempt to haul Zach off Morse but Zach shook off his large second in command as if he were nothing more than a pesky insect.

"Think, man," Chase said, "you won't find out where Allison is from a corpse."

Chase's statement halted Zach where nothing else would. He took several breaths as he glared at Morse, willing himself to regain control. "Where is Sandoval taking her?" The likely place was back to his compound, but Zach wouldn't make assumptions. He had to consider that Sandoval was going after his nuke—if it wasn't at his compound—and taking Allison with him.

Morse slowly slid back along the thick gray carpeting and rested his back against a credenza. He wiped the back of his hand across his bleeding mouth. "No reason not to tell you. Sandoval is going back to South America." Morse lifted one shoulder and let it fall. "Sandoval told me he's taking his wife home."

The compound then. "Why did you do it?" Zach's voice became deadly. "You said you wanted to talk to her. That you thought she might know something about Sandoval. Why did you give her back to him?"

Morse spat blood onto the carpeting and raised an eyebrow in a look devoid of regret or remorse. "It was for the greater good. I was trying to work out a deal with Sandoval. That's why I couldn't have you mess this up by doing a job for him—doing anything—that would make him think he didn't need my help. Sandoval and I have now made that deal. I know he's dirty but he's a small fish. In exchange for returning his wife to him, Sandoval gave up a bigger fish."

Morse had used Allison to close his deal with Sandoval. Zach's fury ignited. "What about the nuke you suspect Sandoval of working on? What about your missing and presumed dead agent?"

"So you know about that, do you?" Morse let out a breath. "We don't have proof of that. What Sandoval provided was hard evidence on a terrorist we've wanted for a long time."

"Well you fucked up, Morse," Zach ground out. "Sandoval has a nuclear weapon and you let him walk."

Morse blanched. "You don't know that for sure."

Morse's door was flung open again and six agents charged into the office. Zach expected them to pounce on him and braced but to his surprise, Morse held up a hand to ward off his men.

"We're fine here," Morse said. "You can all go." When the agents hesitated, Morse shouted, "Get out!" When they were alone again, Morse addressed Zach. "If you know that for sure, you have to tell me." Morse's gaze sharpened and his tone became urgent. "I need to get my people down there."

Zach surged forward. "You stay right here. You've fucked this up enough, Morse. I'm going to get Allison back from Sandoval." Zach's rage became more acute with each breath he took. He bared his teeth in a snarl. "Don't get in my way."

* * *

Allison was seated in Rafael's private plane, across from Rafael. He was watching her, his gaze dark and rabid. She could feel the rage coming off him.

As terrified as she was, if she had it to do over again, she would still have gone with Westwood. By accompanying him, she'd saved Zach and the rest of his men. She clutched her hands in a tight grip thinking of the two men who'd been shot, possibly killed because of her. Guilt and regret weighed down on her. She prayed the two men would recover.

Zach's parting words to her had been that he would come for her. She didn't doubt that he would. She was counting on that, but while she wanted to be back with Zach, wanted nothing more than to be away from Rafael, the thought of what Rafael would do to Zach if he captured him had her blood turning to ice. Rafael would make Zach's death a long, slow, painful one. Allison's heart clutched. She shut her eyes tightly against that horrific thought.

"So quiet, Allison."

Rafael's voice broke the silence.

Allison lifted her gaze to his and gave him the full force of her hatred. "Go to hell." She enunciated carefully, making sure the words came out clearly despite the fierce blow Rafael had given her that had her cheek throbbing like an exposed nerve and had split her lip.

His teeth came together, making a sound she heard though he was seated across from her. "I see you have regained your spirit. We will see how long that lasts once you are back in a cage. Not long at all, I would wager, given your weak nature."

Rafael had drilled that into her, backed by the drugs, undermining her confidence and her belief in herself. She raised her chin. She swiped at the blood on her lip and curled it in disgust at Rafael. "Not so weak that I couldn't get away from you." It felt good to strike back after the months with him when she'd been unable to defend herself, though she knew she'd pay for this bit of defiance.

Rafael's face hardened. "Oh, yes, I am going to enjoy reducing you to the spineless woman you were."

Allison saw the promise in his eyes. He was going to hurt her worse than he had before and this time there would be no getting away. This time she wouldn't survive. She began to shake.

* * *

As soon as they arrived at the compound, Rafael wasted no time putting her back in a cell. One of his men shoved her to the stairs and with his hand fisted in her hair, he pushed her down each step as they made their descent.

The warm South American climate made the temperature below stairs only slightly cooler than elsewhere in the house. Allison was dressed in the warm skirt and sweater she'd donned for the trip to John and should have been perspiring, but goose bumps sprang on her arms. The lower level felt as cold as a freezer to her and she shivered.

Inside the cell, two men who'd accompanied them down there lit lanterns. Rafael turned to a third man, who was as large as a gorilla, and pointed to a table. "There."

Allison kicked and screamed but Rafael's gorilla laid her on the cold, hard table that was centered in the tiny area. Next, the man tore her clothes. The sound of the cloth tearing sounded like shrieks. Naked now, the man grabbed each of her arms and legs in turn.

"No! No!" Allison shouted.

Her heart pounded like a jackhammer. She fought like a wild woman but it was no use. In short order, she was shackled to metal rungs at each corner of the table. Just as the previous table she'd been on, this one was stained with blood. So much blood the table looked painted red. Maybe this was the same table she'd occupied before. Maybe some of the blood coating it was her own and soon would be covered with more of her blood. Hysteria choked her.

This time, Rafael had no concern about leaving marks on her body that may be detected. He went to a wall where instruments of torture hung in a rack and selected one whip and one metal chain. Allison couldn't breathe. Her gaze fixed on the whip Rafael began to gently slap against his palm.

He addressed her for the first time since they'd left the plane. His eyes were black with rage. "You will beg me to kill you."

He flicked the whip against the edge of the table. Allison jumped. Tears pricked her eyes. The first blow struck her belly, leaving a thin trail of blood. The next sliced a thin sliver of skin like a peel from a piece of fruit. Tears filled her eyes and slid off her cheeks. Zach. She tried to focus on Zach and not on the pain. Despite what Rafael had told her, she would not beg him for death. She would live to be with Zach again.

Rafael struck her again. Allison's body arched and then thrashed on the table. Her skin was becoming slick with blood. More blood flowed down her wrists, the shackles cutting her flesh from her desperate attempts to break free.

Rafael shouted questions at her in Spanish. Allison was fluent in the language but pain and terror were overtaking her mind and she could only make out odd words. Strangely, it was the same when he switched to English.

" ... you and Javier ... working with him ... tell you about me ... who else with the CIA ..."

Rafael shouted something else she didn't catch. Two men secured electrodes to various parts of Allison's body. Her breathing hitched. She clawed at the table.

Someone doused the lights. Rafael gave a nod and one man flipped a switch. The electrical current went through her and Allison's body bowed off the table. Her screams echoed in the darkness.

CHAPTER SIXTEEN

Zach studied the Intel spread out on the table before him. Topographical maps. Satellite imagery. Precise coordinates pinpointing the location of Sandoval's compound. Photographs. Zach brushed his thumb across a photo of Allison being dragged into a house that resembled a palace. The expression on her face was one of terror that cut his heart open. *Hang on, baby. I'm coming for you.*

Beside Zach, Chase bent over the table. His mouth was pulled in a thin line. "How do we get this done?"

Zach had to force his gaze away from the photo as if taking his eyes from Allison was abandoning her somehow. Not a chance. He'd do anything—everything—to get her back. Fear for her and what Sandoval was putting her through cut off Zach's breath. His body went cold, in the grip of a fear he'd never known before. He forced himself to regain the control he was fast losing and said to Chase, "Let's figure out the best way in there."

* * *

Twenty four hours later, Zach and his men boarded one of the Corrigan planes. One day wasn't enough time to plan an extraction of this magnitude but Zach couldn't wait any longer. He was out of his mind with fear and worry over what Sandoval was doing to Allison. The one thing he was clinging to was that Sandoval wouldn't kill her right away. Sandoval wouldn't make the same mistake he'd made with Javier by letting his rage rule him and killing Javier before interrogating him.

Sandoval would want to know if Allison had been working with Javier. If she were working for Morse and Morse returned her to Sandoval now to complete her assignment. Sandoval would want to know if there were other CIA plants at his compound.

Zach couldn't think that Allison was already dead. If he did, he'd lose what was left of his mind.

Zach had already been over the plan with his men. They'd fly into South America, take the chopper waiting for them into the jungle, then go from there to Sandoval's front door. It wasn't easy but it would work.

One of Zach's teams was already on the ground doing surveillance. Zach's people would keep an eye on the compound while he was en route so there wouldn't be any surprises when he got there and would provide back up.

Now, here they were. The air felt thick, wet, heavy. It had rained briefly since they'd entered the jungle but the sun and the heat were back quickly. Already they'd burned off the water that dampened the combat wear Zach and his men had on, and glistened on the thick branches and dangling vines. Calls and screeches echoed from the wildlife that inhabited the area.

When they were in range of Sandoval's compound, Zach stopped. Concealed by trees and thick brush, he peered through binoculars at his target. The photos he'd seen of Sandoval's house didn't do it justice. The man had spared no expense to make the place as grand as any monarch and to secure it like a fortress. Zach's Intel had already prepared him for that. His people knew their positions and took them now. Men veered off to the east and west of the compound and would eliminate any threat from those sections. Sandoval was strategic and had towers facing each of the four points. Zach had assigned a sniper for each tower to take out the guards there. Hamilton and Nash broke away to place explosives.

His people were waiting for his signal. Zach gave it and the first sniper took his shot. Within seconds the others followed. Zach watched men drop from the towers and then one explosion after another rocked the earth. He gave the signal to move out. His teams at the east and west sides opened fire. While those men would remain outside, Zach and the men with him now would go into the house.

Automatic weapons fired close to him. Zach returned fire, taking out several men without breaking pace. His path was clear to the defensive wall that surrounded the grounds. No need to scale that wall. The explosives had reduced it to rubble.

Shouts rang out all around him. More gunfire erupted. Chase and his other men joined him at the door. Zach shot off the door and led his men inside.

The foyer was all marble, crystal and gold. Zach had been in a lot of places in all parts of the world but had never seen such opulence. Sandoval had spared no expense to lavish himself in luxury. Sandoval's soldiers ran at Zach and his men from all sides. Zach and his people returned fire and dispatched them.

He spoke into the mic on his shoulder. "We're in. Briggs. Connolly. What's your status?"

"Taking fire from the east," came Connolly's reply.

"Clear here," Briggs said.

"Anyone hurt?" Zach asked.

"Negative," Briggs said.

Connolly responded the same then added, "We'll move to you and Chase and come up behind them."

"Once you've cleared them all," Zach said, "keep an eye out for reinforcements."

"Copy that." Briggs grunted. "No one will get past us."

Zach had no doubt about that. He looked up at the cavernous ceiling. The house was immense. Where was Sandoval keeping Allison? But Zach was afraid he knew.

Zach raised a hand and directed men to search this floor for more of Sandoval's men. He sent others upstairs then led the rest down steep concrete steps to the lower level.

Zach and his men spread out to search the cells. Rats scurried out of the dark. Zach's chest felt as if it were being ripped open, thinking of Allison somewhere down here.

One by one Zach's men reported in. They hadn't found anyone. Allison wasn't in any of the cells. But she had been in one of them until recently. The clothing that Zach had last seen her in lay torn on the floor beneath a blood-stained table. There was blood on the thick metal shackles at each corner of the table. All manner of torture devices were strewn about, scattered as if Sandoval had to move her in a hurry when Zach and his teams breached the compound. All of the instruments of torture held fresh blood. The sight tore a hole through Zach. He staggered but one thing kept him on his feet: He wasn't looking at her dead body. He bowed his head, eyes closed, repeating that to himself. She was alive.

Zach left the cell. Beyond the cells, the ground continued to descend. He hugged the wall and kept his gun raised as he went deeper and deeper into the ground. His men fell in behind him. Cool air rose out of a darkness so thick, he couldn't see his gun hand in front of him. Night vision goggles hung from a strap around his neck and he put them on.

At the bottom, he came to a series of tunnels. Sandoval could not have taken Allison out of here any way other than through one of these tunnels without coming up against Zach's people. But which one?

Chase came up beside Zach. "Any idea where we go from here?"

Zach's gut twisted. He didn't know. He gave the order for his men to split up into pairs and for each pair to go down one of the tunnels.

Mouth tight, Zach said, "Chase, you're with me."

His men went into the tunnels. He and Chase did the same. Zach hadn't realized he was running until Chase's hand clamped down on his shoulder.

Zach was breathing hard. Impatience and fear for Allison rode him. He turned to Chase with a snarl. "Get away from me!"

"Easy, man," Chase said. "You won't be able to find your woman if you're dead."

Zach glared at Chase. Chase's expression didn't ease, telling Zach his own expression had to be murderous. He drew a long breath and brought himself back from the edge. Chase was right. Zach had never advanced like this into the unknown before. Where was the stone-cold resolve he'd always had when carrying out a mission? He'd come to terms with death long ago—his death—not Allison's. Never Allison's. He had to stop thinking that way. He had to think with his head and not like the man who couldn't live without her, or he'd surely overlook something and lose her.

Sandoval and Allison may have gone in this direction alone but that didn't mean they hadn't met up with anyone and were still alone. This tunnel was likely an escape route and Sandoval could have mobilized an army at the end of it.

"I'll lead us in," Zach said.

Chase nodded and stepped back behind Zach. Zach walked on. Each breath brought with it the pungent smell of damp earth. They moved with care not to alert Sandoval of their presence.

Their footsteps were muted by the wet soil that absorbed every footfall. In the tunnel all was quiet, but gunfire could be heard faintly in the distance. Eventually, they began to ascend. Finally, light penetrated the absolute blackness. Zach had been right. The tunnel did lead out. As he neared the end of it, bright sunlight struck him. Zach tore off his goggles and leaving them to dangle around his neck, took the few remaining steps that would bring him to the mouth of the tunnel.

Remaining concealed, he peered out. The tunnel opened onto a dirt road. The road was deserted. The surrounding area was flat land with no places to conceal any army. Sandoval didn't have an army laying in wait. It was just Zach and Chase here.

Zach went outside. They were beyond the walls of Sandoval's compound now. The house was a blur behind them. There was no sign of Sandoval or Allison at all. Zach's fear for Allison escalated. He spoke into his mic, telling his men in the tunnels to backtrack and take the tunnel he and Chase had gone into and to meet up with him and Chase on this road. His men replied they were already almost there. They'd quickly found out that the other tunnels were short and nothing more than decoys that led to dead ends.

Zach ended his communication with his men and stood on the road. "Where did that son of a bitch go with Allison?"

Zach studied the terrain. The road was straight and all around it was strangely cleared of trees and plant life. The only thing here was a cemetery on a small rise. While the earth where Zach and Chase stood was desolate, trees and flowers thrived on the plot of land that housed the cemetery. Sunlight glinted off stately marble monuments that were polished to perfection. A high fence enclosed the area. A single gate towered over the land and bore the inscription: SANDOVAL.

A truck barreled out through the open gate at top speed. Sandoval was behind the wheel. Zach couldn't see Allison but that didn't mean Sandoval didn't have her in back. If she wasn't in the truck, Sandoval knew where she was.

Zach raised his rifle to shoot out the tires and stop the vehicle but hesitated. If Allison was in there with Sandoval, Zach couldn't risk an injury to her. Neither, however, could he let Sandoval take her away.

Zach got the tires in his scope. He was about to shoot them all in rapid succession to bring the vehicle to a complete and immediate stop, when Sandoval appeared to lose control of the vehicle. The truck veered then sideswiped a tree. The vehicle flipped, landing hard on the driver's side.

Allison. Cold sweat broke out over Zach's body as he raced to the truck. Sandoval had gone through the windshield. The passenger side was intact and even before Zach reached it he could see Allison was not inside the vehicle.

Zach vaulted onto the hood of the truck. He raised the butt of his rifle and smashed what was left of the windshield. A thick shard of glass had stabbed Sandoval in the gut, going all the way through his body. Blood streamed from the wound. The man's eyelids were opening and closing. He was barely conscious and Zach knew Sandoval wouldn't survive. Zach wouldn't wait for death to claim Sandoval. Zach would send the bastard to hell himself, but he needed Sandoval to live for one minute more.

Zach seized Sandoval by the throat. "Allison!" Zach shouted. "Where is she?" Sandoval's eyes opened then closed again. Zach squeezed Sandoval's windpipe. "Sandoval!"

Sandoval's dull gaze lifted to Zach and a spark lit there. Sandoval smiled. "Gone. She is gone."

Zach shook Sandoval. "Gone where?" There was a finality in the way Sandoval had said she was gone that started a panic in Zach. "What did you do to her?"

Sandoval moved his lips several times but made no sound. His eyes rolled back in his head. Zach shook Sandoval with a force that had his teeth clacking together. "Where is she? Answer me, you son of a bitch!"

Blood spurted from Sandoval's mouth. His body trembled, then went still. Zach went on shaking him, digging his fists into the now lifeless body. But there were no answers to be gained from Sandoval now.

Zach released him then left the truck. Heart drumming, he faced Chase. "Sandoval left Allison somewhere. We have to find where."

Zach turned away from Chase and headed back in the direction they'd come. Chase ran beside him. Four of Zach's men charged through the tunnel Zach and Chase had come through, and met up with him and Chase on the road. The rest of the men joined them in short order.

Zach stopped in the middle of the road. Allison had been in the tunnel. Right to the end. Where had Sandoval taken her from there?

Sandoval had been at the cemetery. Zach shook his head in denial. But the thought, the fear, wouldn't go away.

"The cemetery." Zach breathed the words. "He left her there."

Blood pounded in Zach's head as he ate up the distance to the cemetery. He moved his head from side to side, looking around wildly.

"Split up," he shouted to his men. "She's here somewhere."

He'd barely finished speaking before he started running. And then he saw it—a freshly dug grave. It was unmarked. Sweet Mother of God, had Sandoval put Allison in there? Zach's heart rate rocketed. He threw his helmet to the ground, fell to his knees in front of the mound of dirt and began clearing away clumps of earth with his hands.

Had Sandoval buried her alive? She was terrified of the dark. He shook his head. None of that mattered if she was already dead. Sweat dripped into his eyes.

He shouted for his men.

"Please. Please. Please." Zach spoke the words aloud, his voice strained and throbbing with emotion. When he got to her, please don't make him be too late.

Zach's men ran to him and dropped to the ground beside him. They dug like they were possessed. No one spoke. Finally, they cleared the dirt from the hole and uncovered a coffin.

"Let me take a look," Chase said.

Zach shook his head, his throat too constricted to verbally respond. His heart was beating so hard it felt like it would beat right out of his chest. He dropped into the hole beside the casket. His hands were sweating, shaking as he lifted the lid. Allison was inside.

She was naked. Bloody. So much blood. Everywhere Zach looked he saw blood. Cuts, welts and burns marred her flesh. Her eyes were open, but they were lifeless.

Zach had to get past the condition of her tortured body and focus on what he needed to do. How long since Sandoval had put her in there? Had he just buried her when Zach spotted him driving out of the cemetery? Air would remain in the casket for a while after burial. Was that time up?

"Allison." Zach's voice came out hoarse.

He tore off his combat gloves and clutched her bloody and bruised face with a hand that shook. Her flesh was still damp from perspiration no doubt brought on by fear and from being in the tight box. She wasn't moving. Wasn't breathing. He pressed his fingertips to her neck. No pulse.

Zach bent over her. He covered her mouth with his and breathed into her.

Dimly, he heard Chase yelling into the mic for Nash, the team medic. Desperate, frantic, Zach took his mouth from Allison's and put his hands on her chest to begin compressions.

"You're not dead." His voice came out choked. "You're not dead."

He did the count, then put his mouth to hers again, forcing more air into her lungs. *Please. Please.* He prayed. He pleaded.

Chase dropped down beside him in the hole. "Take a break. Let me take over."

Zach didn't answer, didn't look up. He forced air into her lungs again. Followed up with more compressions. Over and over Zach repeated the process. Allison remained still.

Zach heard a shout. It sounded like an animal in agony. He realized the sound had come from him. His chest felt torn open. His pain was raw.

Hands shaking, he gripped her face harder as if doing so would keep her with him, keep her from sliding into the void.

He put his mouth to hers again.

Gave her a gust of breath.

Then another.

Another round of compressions.

Another breath.

She remained still.

"Allison ..." he said, his voice broken.

Beneath his mouth, Allison's lips moved.

Zach's heart gave a hard thud, then raced. He raised his head. He stared hard down at her. "Allison. Come on." Breathing hard, he begged,

"Come back to me, baby."

Her gaze remained unfocused. Dull and vacant. Zach knew she wasn't seeing anything. But she was breathing.

He lifted her from the prone position, then out of the casket and into his arms. Her head lolled and he eased it onto his shoulder. She was limp in his arms.

Her body began to tremble. It had to be more than one hundred degrees with the sun beating down on them and she was shaking. He pulled off the protective gear that covered his upper body and stripped off his shirt. He wrapped it around her like a blanket then wrapped his arms around her again.

She needed medical. Nash first and then a hospital. They were still in an unsafe zone. He didn't want to relinquish his hold on any part of her, but he needed to get her out of here. He got to his feet with her in his arms.

"Hand her up to me, Zach," Chase said.

Chase left the hole then reached down and took Allison from Zach. When Zach joined Chase and the others above ground, he took Allison back in his arms. He smoothed her hair that was matted to her skin with sweat, dirt and blood back from her face. She didn't react. She remained still in his arms.

Zach's men surrounded him, shielding Allison from all sides. Clutching her tightly to his chest, Zach ran.

CHAPTER SEVENTEEN

Allison came awake slowly. She opened her eyes and squinted against the light. She was in a bed in a room bright with sunlight. Her eyelids fluttered. She closed her eyes.

"Allison."

Zach. She opened her eyes again and turned her head in the direction of his voice. He was seated on an orange chair pushed close to the bed she was in. He looked like he hadn't shaved or slept in days. He looked so tired. Beyond exhausted. But despite his obvious fatigue, he shot from the chair, his expression urgent.

"Allison." He leaned over her, reaching out slowly to her cheek. His eyes fixed on her as if he hadn't seen her in decades. "No, don't go out again, sweetheart." He swallowed, then again, as if he were struggling to speak. "Stay with me this time."

She continued to stare at him. Was it really Zach or was she imagining him? She recalled the

ambush at the airstrip. Morse giving her to
Rafael. The plane ride to South America. The cell.
The beatings. Rafael flaying her skin with the
whip.

During Rafael's torture, she'd tried to fight
back the pain and the despair by keeping her
mind focused on Zach. Was this one of those
times? Would Zach's image fade when the pain
and fear overrode her defenses and she'd be back
in the cell with Rafael? Her breath caught. "Zach?
Is it really you? Are you real?"

Zach took one of her hands in his. He closed
his eyes for an instant then lowered his head and
pressed his brow to their linked hands. When he
opened his eyes again, they burned into her.
"Yeah. Very real. I'm here, sweetheart. Right here.
And so are you."

Her throat tightened as she took in his words.
Where was here? She realized the bed she was in
was a hospital bed. Not one of Brock's. Panic had
her heart rate jacking up. Where was Rafael? The
last thing she remembered was him putting her
in a coffin. "Rafael buried me alive."

Her breath caught. She was gasping for air as if
she were still in that casket. Zach's arms came
around her as tight as she thought he dared with
her injuries.

"You're safe." Zach pressed his face to her hair.
"You're safe now. I'm not going to let anyone
hurt you."

A tremor coursed through her. "Rafael?"

Zach's jaw tightened. His eyes became
homicidal. "Dead."

Could the devil be killed? But she saw the

truth on Zach's face. Rafael was dead. Tears of relief burned her. She could summon no grief for the man she'd married. That man had never existed. That man had never been real. Rafael had created and adopted a persona to manipulate her and the world. The real man had been a monster. And now that monster was dead. Later, she would ask how he'd died. She wanted that closure, but for now she clung to the fact that he was gone.

"He won't ever hurt you again." Fury burned in Zach's eyes, then again he lowered his brow to their joined hands. When he raised his head again, his eyes were tortured. "I thought I lost you. That I got to you too late." Zach's voice was raw.

She looked up at him. "I knew you'd come for me." Tears gathered and clogged her throat.

Zach cradled her face with both hands. His eyes blazed. "You are my life. I would have gone into hell itself to get you back. You're safe now. No one will ever hurt you again." His face hardened to stone. "Over my dead body will anyone ever hurt you again."

Gently, he brushed hair off her cheek. His gaze lit on each bruise that marred her face. Pain filled his eyes. He touched his lips to her forehead in a kiss so tender, so filled with love, her heart stuttered.

"Let me hold you, Allison." Zach stopped speaking, then swallowed before continuing. "I need to hold you."

Tears streamed down her face. "I need that too."

His hands moved under her gently and he lifted her. His arms came around her and held her against him. She turned her face into his shoulder and curled her arms around his waist, burrowing against him with all the strength she could muster. He held her as if he would hold her forever. She closed her eyes and savored being in his arms, savored being safe.

As if he'd read her mind, Zach said softly against her ear, "You're safe here."

She raised her head only enough to look up at him and kept her tightest grip on his chest. "Where are we?"

Zach pressed his mouth to her fingers. He shook as he kissed her there. "Back in Blake. You're at Blake County General."

"I don't remember getting here."

"You were out of it." Zach closed his eyes for an instant as if the memory of that time was too much for him.

"How long have I been here?"

"Five days."

She didn't remember anything about the journey. "I've been here for five days?"

"Yeah." His voice sounded strangled. "You've been in and out of consciousness."

She hurt everywhere. "How badly am I hurt?"

The tortured look returned to Zach's eyes. "You lost a lot of blood but your doctors said the worst is over. You're going to be all right."

She took a look at herself. Two fingers on the hand Zach wasn't holding were bruised and swollen and taped to a splint. The fingernails were missing. If she looked beneath her hospital gown, she knew what she'd find. Rafael had been thorough. He'd left no part of her untouched.

Rafael was dead but it all came rushing back to her. She was back in that cell with him. Fear and panic overtook her. Tears rushed to her eyes. She began to shake.

Watching her, Zach looked as if his heart were being ripped out of his chest. He was still holding her hand. He released it to wrap both arms around her. "I can't say I know what you're feeling, but you're not alone. I'm here and I'm not going anywhere. I love you. So much. We'll get through this together. Whatever it takes. However long it takes."

Her thoughts and emotions were a mess of pain and uncertainty. She knew Rafael could never hurt her again. *She knew that.* But telling herself that couldn't make the fear go away. She could smell her blood, see her flesh peel, feel her body jerk from the electric current. Bile rose to her throat. She gagged.

Zach reached down for the wastebasket near the nightstand. "Get it out if you need to."

Allison bent over the basket. Zach kept one arm around her and held her hair back with the other. She had nothing in her stomach to come up and her body bucked with dry heaves. Finally, the retching stopped and she fell back against him. She was no longer shaking but she thought that was because her body had used up the last of its strength.

Tears streamed down her cheeks. "I feel like I'm losing myself, Zach."

His arms tightened around her. "I won't let

that happen. I won't let you lose your way. I'll always bring you back to me."

Allison pressed her face hard to his chest. She held tight to his words. Held tight to him. He didn't let go.

* * *

Allison slept the rest of that day and most of the next, but it was good sleep, with no more lapses into unconsciousness.

She opened her eyes to darkness outside the window, though the light overhead kept the room bright. Another night had fallen.

Zach kissed her brow. "Hey."

She blinked up at him. "Hey."

"Is she awake?"

Allison turned at the sound of her mother's voice.

Zach moved his lips from Allison's forehead to her mouth and kissed her carefully, avoiding a deep cut at one corner. He stepped back from the bed and Allison's mother, Linda, eyes streaming tears, took his place. Her mother was a tiny woman but the way she charged to Allison, she would have tried to mow Zach down to get to her.

"My child. My child."

Linda repeated the words as if they were all she was capable of at this moment. Tears fell in a torrent from her eyes. Allison's own eyes filled as her mother took her in her arms. She rocked Allison against her. Linda smelled of her favorite lilac scented bath water. Allison inhaled it deeply, welcoming the familiar scent.

Allison could see her father, Jerry, hovering over her mother's shoulder. Eventually, Linda stepped back and her father came to her bedside. He took in her battered appearance. He wrapped her carefully in his arms and wept as openly as her mother did. Allison couldn't control her own tears.

"I should have taken better care of you," Jerry said. "When time went by and we didn't hear from you, I should have boarded a plane and gone to get you."

Allison shuddered at what Rafael would have done to her father if he'd shown up on his doorstep. "You didn't know, Daddy. You couldn't have known."

"Rafael fooled us all," Jerry said.

By the time her sister Amanda took her turn with Allison, Allison could barely see for all the tears. As she dried her eyes with the backs of her hands, she looked for Zach. He'd stepped back for her to visit with her family, but he hadn't gone far. When she stretched out her arm to him, he took her hand in his. She kept hold of his hand and tugged him into the circle made by her parents, her sister and herself. With Zach included, the circle now felt complete.

Allison began to make introductions.

Zach kissed her palm. "We've all met, sweetheart. Chase picked up your parents from the airport. They've been here everyday waiting for you to wake up."

Linda raised a hand and gently brushed Allison's brow. "Mr. Chase explained to us how

Zach and his people took you away from Rafael." Tears welled in Linda's eyes again and she raised her gaze to Zach. "We can never thank you for all you did."

Zach's gaze left Linda. He looked to Allison and his eyes warmed. "She's here and she's safe. I don't need anything more than that."

Her parents stayed to visit until Allison's strength began to visibly fade, then they got to their feet.

"We'll be back in the morning, darling," Linda said.

First her mother then her father kissed her again and they took their leave.

Amanda lingered after their parents left. "I have a feeling we're going to be seeing a lot of you, Zach."

Zach bent and kissed the top of Allison's head softly. "If I have anything to say about it."

Amanda gave Zach a stern look that was belied by a one-sided smile. "I like you. Don't make me regret it."

Zach laughed. "I'll do my best."

Amanda hugged Allison. "Love you, sis."

"You, too," Allison said returning her sister's embrace.

Amanda broke her grip on Allison then turned to Zach and wound her arms around him. She blinked back tears. "Take good care of my sister."

"Always." Zach's tone was fierce.

Amanda left the room to join their parents. Zach resumed his seat.

Allison reached out and laced her fingers through his. "You need more sleep than you're getting in that chair."

Zach lowered his head and kissed her hand where it joined his. "I'm fine now that I know you're going to be all right."

She could see the truth of his words in his eyes. How she loved this man. He'd risked everything to make her safe. But her safety hadn't come without cost. "How are Braddock and McMurtry?"

Zach smiled. "Recovering. They're going to be fine."

Allison closed her eyes. "Thank God." She held her breath. "Rafael's weapon? Did you find it?"

Zach nodded. "One of my teams found a safe where Sandoval kept information. They found the location of the nuke. John has it. You can rest easy, sweetheart. That weapon is no longer a threat. Without Sandoval, his regime is falling apart. Soon it will be gone completely."

"I can't believe it's really, finally over."

"Believe it. You stopped him. We can add that to the list of things we have to be thankful for this year."

Thanksgiving. "I thought I'd missed Thanksgiving this year." She bit her lip. She hadn't been certain she'd ever enjoy another Thanksgiving again. Zach was right. They had so much to be thankful for. "What's today's date?"

Zach caressed her hair then her face. "Thanksgiving is the day after tomorrow. If you're feeling up to it, and if the doctors agree, we can spend it with both our families. My folks, Ed and Ellen, know your parents and sister are in Blake and have invited them to join us all at their house. If you're not feeling up to it, we'll sit this year out. Spend it at my place or right here in this room. Just the two of us. Whatever you want, I'll do."

Allison didn't have to think before making that decision. "I want us all to be together."

Zach kissed her forehead softly, keeping his lips there. "Then that's what you'll have."

CHAPTER EIGHTEEN

Allison got the go ahead from her doctor to leave the hospital for Thanksgiving and two days later, she, her parents and sister stepped out of Zach's SUV onto the Turner's driveway. With her hand tucked tightly in Zach's, Allison followed him into the Turner home.

The front door opened into a tiny hall that branched off to a combination living and dining room. The kitchen was at the back of the house and wholly visible from the entrance. Steam rose from pots on the stove and filled the home with a heavenly aroma.

The house was small, made smaller by all the people crowded into the tight space. Men and women stood against off-white plaster walls and sat on worn couches and an assortment of chairs that looked to have been brought in to accommodate the large number of bodies. Children played everywhere. Everyone seemed to be talking and laughing at once and the noise level was just below a roar.

Zach added his voice to the noise with a shout. "Hey!"

Somehow he was heard. Heads turned in their direction. People broke away from their conversations and met them at the door to greet them. A woman with silver hair that flowed beautifully to her shoulders pushed through and made her way to Zach.

Her eyes were all on Zach. She broke into a huge smile as she looked up at him. She rose on tiptoe. Zach bent and she flung her arms around his neck in a fierce hug. Zach curled his arms around her waist, returning her embrace with one that was just as enthusiastic.

"I'm so glad you're back home." The woman's voice was thick as if she were on the verge of tears.

"Me, too," Zach said.

Allison noticed Zach's voice had gone a little thick as well.

After a moment, Zach took one arm from around the woman. He draped it around Allison's shoulders and brought her to his side. "Allison, I'd like you to meet my mother, Ellen Turner. Mom, this is Allison."

Allison hadn't needed the introduction. She'd known this woman was Ellen by the love in Zach's eyes. Nerves fluttered in Allison's stomach at meeting the woman who meant so much to Zach he considered her his mother. But an instant later, Allison realized her nerves were unnecessary.

Ellen gave Allison a warm hug. "Welcome,

Allison. I'll let you in on a secret. Zach's never brought a woman to our Thanksgivings. You must be very special to him. I'm looking forward to getting to know you."

Allison was warmed by Ellen's kind welcome. "Thank you. I feel the same about you."

Still holding Allison to her, Ellen said, "Come. Let's find you a place to sit and while you're seated, I'll fill a plate for you with appetizers."

Before they'd taken a step, a man leaning heavily on a thick-pronged cane, reached them. Moving with obvious difficulty, he drew Zach into a tight embrace.

"Hey, Pop." Zach hugged the other man for a long moment before stepping back. "Pop, this is—"

"I heard." He took Allison's uninjured hand in his. "I'm Ed Turner, young lady. Make yourself at home."

The man had a gravelly voice that sounded gruff. On sight, he appeared stern, but his eyes crinkled with his smile and showed kindness and warmth. Allison liked him at once. "Thank you for inviting me to be here with you and your family."

Ed gave her hand a squeeze. "I heard Ellen say something about getting you a seat. Let's do that."

Zach plopped a hand on Ed's shoulders. "I'll find Allison a seat, Pop. I'd like you and Mom to say hello to Allison's parents, Jerry and Linda, and Allison's sister, Amanda."

Allison's family was standing behind Zach and Allison. Zach turned to them and made the introductions. Ed and Ellen welcomed them. Jerry, Linda and Amanda were not shy butterflies and as Zach led Allison deeper into the house, she heard them all already engaged in conversation.

"Now that wasn't too bad." Zach winked at her.

But Allison was no longer looking at Zach. There, in the crowd, she saw ... Rafael. She gasped then blinked. The man's face came into focus. Of course it wasn't Rafael but perspiration bathed her body and she was now breathing hard.

Zach drew them to a stop in the middle of the living room and turned to face her. His eyes showed alarm. "Allison? What is it?"

She swallowed back her fear. "Nothing." When Zach didn't look convinced she added, "Really, I'm fine."

Zach watched her steadily for a time before his taut features eased. He resumed their walk through the crowd, stopping to introduce Allison to people along the way. She focused her attention on the people she was meeting. A man named Harwick. A woman who introduced herself as Kelly McNamara. More Turners, aunts, uncles and a host of cousins. Each step brought a new person. So many people. So many names. It was like the first day teaching her fifth graders. She didn't know how she'd remember them all. But she always did.

The memory was a fond one. She loved teaching. Missed teaching. Rafael had told her she could teach in his country. But that never happened. Instead, she'd found herself married to the devil himself.

Allison's stomach churned. She closed her eyes and licked her now dry lips, fighting to push back the thought and bring herself back to the here and now.

Taking deep breaths, she reopened her eyes and forced her attention back to the present. In the present, she was celebrating Thanksgiving with the man she loved and both their families. She latched onto that but the memory had started her heart beating hard and left her chilled.

Zach slowly wended their way through the crowd. She couldn't see over most of the people in front of her and just followed Zach blindly along. Four men came toward them. She couldn't miss them. They were all big men. Zach brought them to a stop and Allison was introduced to Mitch and Ben Turner, John Burke, and Gage Broderick, the men Zach called his brothers.

Mitch was the first to come to her. He kissed her softly on one cheek where the bruises had faded to yellow.

"Welcome, Allison," Mitch said.

Each of the other men also kissed her cheek and offered greetings. Seeing them all together, it was obvious these men cared as deeply for Zach as he did for them.

"Where are your ladies?"

Zach's voice broke into her thoughts. He was addressing Mitch, Ben, Gage and John.

"In our old room," Mitch said. "Trying to get Sara to take a nap before we eat." Mitch turned to include Allison. "Sara's my daughter."

Allison acknowledged the information with a nod. She recalled Zach mentioning Sara, and

Mitch's impending adoption of her when he'd told her of his family. The way Mitch's eyes warmed when he spoke of the little girl, it was obvious he loved her very much.

"She okay?" Zach asked. It was clear by his tone that he cared for the child.

Mitch laughed. "Oh, yeah. She's just not having any part of taking a nap."

"Having my boys in there with her can't be helping," Ben said.

Zach had told Allison that Ben had two sons, both under two years old.

Zach laughed at Ben's remark then looked around. "Where's Ryan?"

The humor left the other mens' faces at once.

"Not coming," Gage said.

Zach's mouth firmed. "More trouble with Tina?"

"Yeah," Mitch said, his own mouth now tight. "We need to all go down there and see him as soon as possible."

They all agreed.

Zach hissed a slow breath. He was clearly angry and concerned at his friend Ryan's situation.

Zach turned to Allison. Gently, he rubbed a hand up then down her arm. "Wait here with my brothers, sweetheart. I'll get you that chair."

* * *

After the meal was eaten and everyone helped with the clean up, Allison broke away from the gathering. She opened the kitchen door and stepped onto the snow-covered back porch she'd glimpsed while drying dishes sitting at the table, the only way Ellen, in her kind concern for Allison, had allowed Allison to help.

Allison stood in a drift of snow looking out at the moon-kissed yard and the tightly-grouped houses beyond, all brightly lit for the holidays. The night air was still with no wind but cold.

She hadn't been outside long when she heard the kitchen door open again. Zach came up behind her. He draped her jacket around her shoulders then pressed her back to his front and put his arms around her, warming her further.

He rested his chin on top of her head. "You forgot your jacket."

She glanced over her shoulder at him. "You're not wearing a jacket."

"That's different."

"Badass, huh?"

"You got it."

She smiled but she couldn't get into the mood of his teasing and her smile faded quickly. Her mind was a jumble and her body was tense.

Zach turned her slowly in his arms. "You hardly ate. What's on your mind, baby? Was this too much? Too many people?"

She was quick to shake her head and alleviate his worry. "No. They're great."

He rubbed his thumb gently across her cheek. "Then what is it, sweetheart?"

He was looking at her with so much love that it made her feel a little weak. And a lot afraid. She didn't want to ruin this happy time with his family for him and that was why she'd come out to be by herself. She realized she wasn't doing a good job of hiding her feelings since he'd come out here after her.

Zach gently tipped up her chin, bringing her gaze to his. "Hey. Where are you? In your head, where'd you go?"

She tried to turn away but he wouldn't let her. It all became too much. She blurted out her worst fear. "Why do you want me? I'm a disaster. I don't know if I'll ever not be a disaster again."

"Allison—"

"No, listen to me." She grasped his arms tightly, digging her finger nails into his skin. "In the house when we walked in, I thought one of the people was Rafael. Later, while meeting your family and friends, I thought of my fifth graders and that happy thought morphed into an ugly thought of Rafael.

"Rafael is gone. It's over but he's still inside my head. I don't even need to close my eyes to be back with him, reliving the pain and the fear and the helplessness that I was unable to save myself." Her breath was coming so fast she choked on the words. "I'll have the scars from Rafael's torture for the rest of my life. You were there when the doctor said that. You heard him. The scars will forever be a visual reminder. I won't be able to look at myself without thinking of Rafael and what he did to me. And neither will you." A bone-deep coldness seeped into her. One she feared would never go away. She started shaking. "I can't get Rafael out of me. I don't know if I'll ever be able to. You need to run away from me, Zach." Her voice broke. "Run as fast as you can."

Zach's expression darkened. His anger was obvious though just as obvious was that he wasn't angry at her. He didn't respond right away but closed his eyes for a moment as if he couldn't go on, as if he were calling on his strength to be able to continue without losing his composure.

He reached out and held her cheek softly. "I hate that you have those scars but not because of the way they make you look but because Sandoval hurt you. And now, though that physical pain you suffered is over, those scars are continuing to hurt you emotionally just by their very presence.

"I hate that Sandoval still has the power to cause you pain. I'd like to drag him back from hell and into that cell of his and do to him everything he did to hurt you. And then I'd hand him over to you to finish the job so you'd know you aren't powerless against him. You aren't helpless. You never were. You took everything he did to you and you still had the courage and the will to survive.

"It kills me thinking of what you suffered." Zach's voice filled with pain. "To see you still suffering." His hold on her cheek tightened fractionally. "Get this: I am not going away. Every time you think of that son of a bitch, I'm going to tell you and show you how much I love you. That bastard may be in your head now but I'm going to force him out and I'll keep forcing him out for as long as it takes to get him out for good."

Allison stared up at him, at the strength and

the resolve in his eyes. And the love. Her lips trembled. She echoed his words from earlier. "I love you. So much." Tears blurred her vision of him.

Zach gently brushed his thumbs over the tears trailing down her cheeks. "So much." Mindful of her injuries, he wrapped his arms gently around her. He brought his mouth softly to hers. "So much," he repeated. "And always."

TURN THE PAGE FOR A SPECIAL
PREVIEW OF KAREN FENECH'S NEXT
PROTECTORS NOVEL

GUILTY

COMING SOON TO EBOOK
AND PAPERBACK

CHAPTER ONE

"Agent Winston, how do you feel knowing you put a murderer back on the streets?"

FBI Special Agent Faith Winston closed her eyes briefly as the question struck home. It was shouted at her from one of the throng of television and newspaper reporters gathered on the steps of the Manhattan County District Courthouse.

Rain pelted the ground, soaking the hair and the suit jackets of the men and women surrounding her. In anticipation of her response to their colleague's question, the crowd moved closer. Faith took a breath and inhaled the odor of damp clothing. Tightening her grip on the handle of her suitcase, she pulled the luggage, making it bounce down the concrete steps, then she pushed through the crowd. Somewhere beyond this mass of people was the taxi she'd called to take her to JFK airport.

"Agent Winston what's going through your mind now, knowing that if not for you, a young woman would still be alive?"

Guilt stabbed her as Faith blinked rain from her eyes and brought the trim redhead who'd spoken into focus. The reporter clutched a microphone that displayed the prominent *Eye On Manhattan* logo. She stepped out from beneath the shelter of a chrome-tipped umbrella and jabbed the microphone at Faith.

Faith had just spent forty-five minutes on the

witness stand providing details of her role in setting a murderer free. There was nothing more to be said now. Nothing she could or would say to try to exonerate herself. She turned away from the mic, jostled the man beside her and continued down the steps. She was almost to the sidewalk now. The crowd continued to move with her as tight as a swarm of bees. She couldn't see beyond her own feet. It was because of her familiarity with the courthouse that she knew where she was.

Cries and shouts rang out behind her.

"Mr. Fahey! Mr. Fahey how do you feel about Agent Winston's testimony?"

Timothy Fahey. It was the murder of his sister Sharon that had brought them all to the courthouse today.

At the appearance of Timothy Fahey, the reporters scattered, running back up the steps. At last, an opening. And beyond, Faith spotted a yellow taxi parked at the curb, engine idling.

Fahey's voice boomed across the courtyard. "Rather than answer that question, I'd like to ask one of my own. To Agent Winston. How can you live with yourself?"

His voice resonated with anger and pain that struck Faith like a physical blow. Again, guilt stabbed her. But his words elicited more than guilt as they penetrated her to her core. Fahey had lost the last of his family. Faith knew what it was to have no family. To be completely alone in the world. Just as Fahey was now.

Sharon had been Timothy Fahey's last living relative. They'd shared an apartment since the death of their parents when Fahey was eighteen and Sharon, fifteen. Fahey had been the one to discover Sharon's body when he'd returned home at the end of a work day.

One of the reporters broke away from Fahey and taking the descent two steps at a time, raced back to Faith. "Agent Winston will you answer Mr. Fahey's question? Agent Winston!"

Faith reached the taxi and swung open the rear passenger door. She climbed in, hoisting the suitcase up onto the vinyl seat with her. Static rose from the dispatch radio inside the cab, punctuated by squeaks from the windshield wipers as they arced across the glass. The cabbie turned to face Faith, bracing his arm across the seat. A tattoo on his bicep proclaimed him as *#1 Mets Fan*.

"Where to, lady?" he asked in an accent that was thick South Bronx.

"JFK."

Faith closed the car door. Almost immediately it was flung open.

"I already got a fare. You blind, mac!" the cabbie yelled.

The newcomer held up his NYPD badge. Detective Joe Colson.

Colson addressed the cabbie. "Can you give us a minute?"

The cabbie groaned. "C'mon man, I'm trying to make a living here!" But he flung up his arms and left the vehicle.

Colson got inside the car and sat beside Faith. He was not a huge man, but needed more than the small amount of space that Faith and her suitcase did not occupy. He shifted position. It was not a comfortable fit for him, or for Faith either as his body now brushed hers.

He eyed Faith. "I worked the Fahey homicide."

"What do you want?"

The detective puckered his lips as if in contemplation. "I wouldn't turn down a boat that I could sail around the world in." He swiped the heel of his hand across the rain trickling down his face. "But for right now, I'd settle for a word with you." His expression hardened. "It's on your head that woman is dead."

Faith sat in silence. Colson was right. If not for her involvement, Sharon Fahey would still be alive.

"He got better at killing," Colson went on. "Didn't leave any trace evidence behind this time that we can use to nail him. Our case is nothing more than smoke and mirrors. It's a good bet he's going to walk." Colson leaned toward her, close enough for Faith to smell his breath. A blend of coffee and chocolate. "I'd wish you a good flight home," he said, "but I'd be lying."

Colson left the vehicle, slamming the door.

The cab driver returned. "Just so you know, I'm expecting a big tip on account of you putting me out like this, lady."

Without waiting for a response, he pulled away from the curb and joined the late afternoon traffic. A horn honked. The cabbie leaned on his own horn and flipped a trucker the bird.

Timothy Fahey's question returned to her.

How can you live with yourself?

Faith faced the window, where rain ran in

rivulets down the glass, and wondered the same thing.

If you'd like to know when the next Protectors novel is released, sign up for Karen Fenech's notification-only news at her website: www.karenfenech.com

Or type this direct link into your browser: http://ymlp.com/xgeubjejgmguu

ABOUT THE AUTHOR

USA Today Bestselling Author Karen Fenech writes romantic suspense novels and short works of suspense. She is the author of the romantic suspense series, The Protectors. Karen's novels and short suspense fiction have received critical acclaim and have been translated into several languages. When Karen's not writing or spending time with her family, she loves to shop, watch movies, and just kick back in a comfortable chair and read.

You can reach Karen here:

Facebook:
http://www.facebook.com/KarenFenechsFriends
Twitter:
https://twitter.com/karenfenech
Website:
http://www.karenfenech.com

If you'd like to know when Karen Fenech's next novel is released, sign up for her notification-only news at her website: www.karenfenech.com

PRAISE FOR THE BESTSELLING NOVELS OF KAREN FENECH

{GONE} "Karen Fenech's GONE is a real page turner front to back. You won't be able to put this one down!" —NEW YORK TIMES BESTSELLING AUTHOR KAT MARTIN

{GONE} "Karen Fenech tells a taut tale with great characters and lots of twists. This is a writer you need to read." —USA TODAY BESTSELLING AUTHOR MAUREEN CHILD

{GONE} "Readers will find themselves in the grip of GONE as this riveting tale plays out. GONE is a provocative thriller filled with a roller coaster ride that carries the suspense until the last page." —DEBORAH C. JACKSON, ROMANCE REVIEWS TODAY

{BETRAYAL} "An excellent read." —DONNA M. BROWN, ROMANTIC TIMES MAGAZINE

{IMPOSTER: The Protectors Series — Book One} "IMPOSTER is romantic suspense at its best!" —USA TODAY BESTSELLING AUTHOR MAUREEN CHILD

{UNHOLY ANGELS} "... a superbly intricate tale of greed, power, and murder... a suspenseful and believable story that will keep you reading into the wee hours of the morning. Highly recommended!"— BESTSELLING AUTHOR D.B. HENSON

NOVELS BY KAREN FENECH

Betrayal

Gone

Unholy Angels

Imposter: The Protectors Series — Book One

Snowbound: The Protectors Series — Book Two

Pursued: The Protectors Series — Book Three

Hide: The Protectors Series — Book Four

Three Short Stories Of Suspense: Deadly
Thoughts, Secrets & The Plan

Made in the USA
Coppell, TX
19 August 2023

20537005R00144